On a driven groan Luiz turned back to the bedroom.

His dark lashes drifted downward as he looked Caroline over. She looked pagan, uninhibitedly wanton. A bride ready for the taking by her passionate Spanish husband.

Allowing her feet to touch the floor, Luiz took a step back then began undressing. Caroline didn't move, didn't attempt to take her own dress off. It was his duty to unwrap his bride himself.

But all the while he was undressing, the moist pink tip of her tongue kept on touching her kiss-swollen lips in needy anticipation.

"You ought to be locked up," he murmured when he eventually reached for her. She just smiled a very wicked smile. Her dress slipped lower. On a growl, Luiz helped it the rest of the way.

Michelle Reid

THE SPANISH HUSBAND

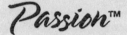

Passion™

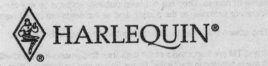

HARLEQUIN®

TORONTO • NEW YORK • LONDON
AMSTERDAM • PARIS • SYDNEY • HAMBURG
STOCKHOLM • ATHENS • TOKYO • MILAN • MADRID
PRAGUE • WARSAW • BUDAPEST • AUCKLAND

ISBN 0-373-12145-8

THE SPANISH HUSBAND

First North American Publication 2000.

CHAPTER ONE

CAROLINE was pacing the floor and becoming more agitated with each step that she took. She arrived at the window which led out onto the terrace, saw nothing of the beautiful view the elegant two-bedroom suite offered her of the famous Puerto Banus, and turned to pace back the way she had come, glancing impatiently at her watch as she did so.

Nine o'clock. Her father had said seven o'clock. He had *promised* seven o'clock. 'Just going for a stroll before I need to change for dinner,' he'd said. 'To check out the old place and see if it's changed much since we were here last.'

He loved Marbella. They'd used to spend most of their summers here once upon a time, so she'd understood his eagerness to reacquaint himself with the resort—but not his refusal to let her go with him.

'Don't be a pain, Caroline,' he'd censured when she'd instantly started to get anxious. 'I don't need you to hold my hand. And I certainly don't need a watchdog. Show a little faith, for goodness' sake. Haven't I promised to behave myself?'

So she'd showed a little faith—and now look at her, she mocked herself bitterly. For here she was, pacing the floor like a worried mother hen with every nerve-end she possessed singing out a warning of trouble!

He wouldn't let her down—would he? She tried to reassure herself. He had been so firm, so *needy* for her to believe in him that he wouldn't, surely, fall prey to his old

5

weakness when he knew how important it was to them for him to remain strong?

Then where is he? A very cynical voice inside her head taunted. He's been gone for hours. And you know what he can get up to when left to his own devices for too long.

'Oh, hell,' she muttered as the agitation suddenly reached whole new levels, and, in tight and angry surrender to it, she snatched up her little black velvet evening bag and headed for the suite's outer door.

If she discovered that he had sneaked off to feed his damned habit then she would never forgive him! She vowed as she stabbed a hard finger at the lift call button then stood waiting impatiently for it to come. Things were bad enough already.

More than bad enough, she groaned inwardly. Or she wouldn't even be here, her father knew that! He knew how much she hated this place now, hated the whole morass of painful emotions it evoked.

Seven years since their last visit, she recalled as the lift doors slid open. Seven years since they had been forced to leave beneath a dark cloud of pride-shrivelling humiliation and soul-destroying heartbreak, vowing never to return again.

Yet here they were, not only back in Marbella but staying in the same hotel. And once again she was having to go and hunt her father out in the very last place on this earth she ever wanted to step foot in!

The casino, she named it grimly as she walked into the lift. The wretched in-house casino, where she was all too aware of the damage her father could do in such a terrifyingly short space of time.

And how long had he been missing? she asked herself as she pressed for the ground floor.

Two hours at least.

Her fingers stood out white against her black evening

bag while she waited for the lift doors to shut. In two miserable hours he could lose thousands. Give him a whole night and he would, quite happily, lose his shirt!

Like the last time.

A wave of sickness suddenly washed over her, sending her slumping weakly against the lift wall just as the doors began to close. A hand snaked out, compelling the doors to open again, and she found herself quickly straightening as a tall dark man of Spanish descent, dressed in an impeccably tailored black dinner suit and bow tie, stepped lithely into the cabin with her.

'My apologies for delaying you,' he murmured in smoothly modulated English, swinging round to offer her a smile. A smile that instantly arrested when his eyes actually focused on her.

'That's okay,' she replied, and quickly dropped her gaze so as not to encourage any further contact.

The lift began to sink. Standing tensely by the console, Caroline was stingingly aware that he was still studying her, but pretended not to notice. It wasn't a new experience for her to be looked at like this. She had the kind of natural blonde, curvaceously slender, long-legged figure that incited men to stare. And the stranger was good-looking; she had noticed that about him before she'd lowered her gaze.

But she was in no mood to be chatted up in a lift—if she was ever in the mood anywhere, she then added, bleakly aware that it had been a long time since she had let any man get close to her.

Not since Luiz, in fact, right here in Marbella.

Then. No. Abruptly she severed that memory before it had a chance to get a grip. She wasn't going to think of Luiz. It was a promise she had made to herself before she came here. Luiz belonged in the distant past, along with every other bitter memory Marbella had the power to throw up at her. And this tall dark stranger looked too much like Luiz to stand the remotest chance with her.

So she was relieved when the lift stopped and she could escape his intense regard without him attempting to make conversation. Within seconds she had completely forgotten him, her mind back on the problem of finding her father as she paused at the head of a shallow set of steps which led down to the main foyer and began searching the busy area in front of her.

This was one of the more impressive hotels that stood in prime position on Marbella's Puerto Banus. Years ago, the hotel had possessed a well-earned reputation for old-fashioned grandeur which had made it appeal to a certain kind of guest—a select kind that had once included both herself and her father.

But the hotel had only just been re-opened, after a huge refurbishment undertaken by its new owners, and although it still held pride of place as one of the most exclusive hotels in the resort, it now displayed its five-star deluxe ranking with more subtle elegance.

And the people were different, less rigidly correct and aware of their own status, though she didn't doubt for a moment that if they were staying here then they must be able to afford the frankly extortionate rates.

It was a thought that brought home to her just how much she had changed in seven years. For seven years ago she too would not have so much as questioned the price of a two-bedroom suite in any hotel. She had been reared to expect the best, and if the best came with a big price-tag attached to it then that was life as she had known it.

These days she didn't just question price-tags, she calculated how long she would have to work to make that kind of money.

In fact money was now an obsession with Caroline. Or at least the lack of it was, along with a constant need to keep on feeding that greedy monster her family home had become.

A frown touched her brow as she continued to search for the familiar sight of her father's very distinctive tall and slender figure among the clutches of people gathered in the foyer. For two hundred years there had been Newburys in residence at Highbrook Manor. But the chances of there being Newburys there for very much longer depended almost entirely on what her father was doing at this precise moment.

And he certainly wasn't in evidence here, she acknowledged as, with a grace that belied her inner tension, she set herself moving down the steps and across the foyer to see if he had left a message for her at the reception desk.

He hadn't. Next she went off to check out the lounge bars in the faint hope that he might have met someone he'd used to know, got to talking and lost track of the time. Again she drew a blank, and her heart began to take on a slower, thicker beat because she knew that there was now only one place left for her to look for him.

Grimly she set her feet moving over to a flight of steps set in their own discreet alcove that led the way down to the hotel basement. Walking down those steps took a kind of courage no one would understand unless they had known her seven years ago. By the time she reached the bottom she was even trembling slightly. For very little had changed down here except maybe the decoration, she noticed with a sickly feeling of *déjà vu*. The basement area still possessed its own very stylish foyer, still had a sign pointing to the left directing the guests to the hotel's fully equipped gymnasium, beauty therapy rooms and indoor swimming pool.

Still had a pair of doors to her right, which were as firmly closed as they always had been, as if to keep carefully hidden from innocent eyes what went on behind them.

But the sign hanging above the doors was not innocent. 'Casino' it announced in discreet gold lettering.

Her father's favourite playground of old, she thought with a small shiver. A place where compulsive excitement went hand in hand with desperation and the flip of a card or the roll of a dice or the spin of a wheel had the potential to make or break you.

If he had given in to himself and gone in search of excitement, then she was sure she was going to find him on the other side of those wretched doors, she predicted as she took a reluctant step forward.

'You will be disappointed,' a smoothly accented voice drawled lazily.

Spinning round in surprise, Caroline found herself looking at the stranger who had shared the lift with her. Tall, dark, undeniably good-looking—her stomach muscles flipped on yet another sense of *déjà vu*. For he really did look uncannily like Luiz. The same age, the same build, the same rich Spanish colouring.

'I beg your pardon?' she said, thinking that even her first meeting with Luiz had been right here in this basement foyer, with her hovering uncertainly like this and him smiling at her like that...

'The casino,' he prompted with a nod of his dark head in the direction of the closed doors. 'It does not open until ten o'clock. You are too early...'

Pure instinct made her check the time on her watch, to discover that it was only nine-fifteen. Sheer relief had her winging a warm smile at the stranger—because if the casino wasn't even open, then her father could not be ensconced in there, wrecking what small chance they had of saving their home!

And now she felt guilty. Guilty for mistrusting him,

guilty for being angry, guilty for thinking the worst of him when of course he wouldn't do that to her!

'Perhaps I could persuade you to share a glass of wine with me in the lounge bar, while we wait for the casino to open?' the stranger invited.

Caroline flushed, realising that he had misinterpreted her sudden smile, and the pick-up she had carefully avoided in the lift was back on track with a vengeance. The kind of vengeance that made him flash her a megawatt smile.

By contrast she completely froze him. 'Thank you, but I am here with someone,' she informed him stiffly, and pointedly turned back to the stairs.

'Your father, Sir Edward Newbury, perhaps?' he suggested lightly, successfully bringing her departure to a halt.

'You know my father?' she questioned warily.

'We have met,' he smiled. But it was the way that he smiled that chilled Caroline's blood. As if he knew something she didn't and was deriding that knowledge.

Or deriding her father.

'I have just seen him,' he added. 'He crossed the foyer towards the lifts only a few short minutes ago. He seemed—in a hurry...' That lazily mocking smile appeared again, making her feel distinctly uneasy.

'Thank you,' she said politely. 'For letting me know.' And she turned away from him once again.

The feel of his fingers closing around her wrist came as a shock. 'Don't rush away,' he murmured. 'I would really like to get to know you better...'

His voice was quite pleasantly pitched—but his grip was an intrusion and alarm bells were beginning to sound in her head, because she had a horrible feeling that if she tried to break free his fingers would tighten—painfully.

She didn't like this man, she decided. She didn't like his smooth good-looks or his easy confidence or the lazy charm he was utilising—while using physical means to detain her.

She didn't like his touch on her skin, or the itchy suspicion that he had been shadowing her movements since the lift, and had timed his approach to coincide with the fact that they were standing at the bottom of a flight of stairs well away from other people.

And she didn't like the uneasy sensation of feeling vulnerable to someone stronger than herself and clearly so sure of himself that he dared detain her like this.

'Please let go of me,' she said.

His grip did tighten. Her pulse began to accelerate. 'But if I let you go you will not learn *how* I became acquainted with your papa,' he pointed out. 'Or, perhaps more significantly, *where* I became acquainted with him...'

'Where?' she responded, aware that he was deliberately dangling the knowledge at her like a carrot on a stick.

'Share a glass of wine with me,' he urged. 'And I will tell you.'

And it was such a juicy carrot, she noted, one that was trying to make her go one way while every single instinct she possessed was telling her to run in the other.

At which point anger took over, for if he believed she was open to this kind of coercion then he was severely mistaken! 'I'm sure,' she replied in her coldest voice, 'that if my father thinks your meeting memorable enough he will tell me about it himself. Now, if you will excuse me?' she concluded, and gave a hard enough tug at her captured wrist to free it, then walked stiffly up the steps without glancing back.

But her insides felt shaky, and the nerves running along her spine were tingling, because she half expected him to come chasing after her. It was an unpleasant sensation, one that stayed with her all the way up that flight of steps and across the busy foyer into one of the waiting lifts. In fact it was only when the doors had shut her in without him joining her there that she began to feel safe again.

And her wrist hurt. Glancing down at it, she wasn't surprised to find the delicate white skin covering it was showing the beginnings of bruising. Who was he? she wondered. What was he to her father that made him believe it was okay to accost her like that?

It was a concern that took her into her suite and immediately across to her father's bedroom door with the grim intention of finding out. But, having knocked sharply and then pushed open the door, she knew she was going to be unlucky, when it became immediately apparent that he had already been here and gone again.

And the way his clothes had been discarded on the floor told her he had changed in one heck of a hurry.

So as to avoid her? Oh, yes, Caroline conceded heavily. He was trying to avoid her—which could only mean one thing.

He had fallen off the rails again.

In a fit of angry frustration she bent down to snatch up the pair of trousers he had dropped on the floor and was about to toss them onto the bed when something dropped out of one of the pockets. It landed with a paper-like thud on the toe of her shoe. Bending to pick it up, she discovered that she was holding what appeared to be a set of receipts, and with her fingers actually tingling with dread, she slowly unfurled them.

After that she didn't move, didn't breathe, didn't even think a coherent thought for long, long seconds. Then, with a calmness that bore no resemblance to what was actually taking place inside her, she began to check with the methodical intent of one well-practised at doing it, every pocket in every item of clothing he had brought with him to Marbella.

Ten minutes later and she was standing there in the middle of her father's room, staring into space like someone turned to stone. They had been here in Marbella for less than twenty-four hours and, going by the tally on the receipts, in that time her father had managed to gamble and lose the best part of one hundred thousand pounds...

Standing by the window of his hi-tech control room, Luiz Vazquez looked down on the casino floor of this, the latest acquisition in his growing string of deluxe hotels.

He could not be seen from down on the floor. The window allowed him to look out but did not let anyone look in. And behind him the really serious viewing was going on, via closed circuit television screens watched over by his eagle-eyed security staff. The window was merely a secondary source by which the casino floor as a whole could be observed.

Luiz preferred to check out the floor with his own eyes like this. It came from once being a serious gambler and trusting nothing he could not see for himself. Now things were different. Now he didn't need to gamble to earn enough money to live. He had wealth and he had power and a kind of deeply satisfying sense of self-respect that had taken a whole lot of earning and yet...

A frown brought the two dark silk strips of his brows together across the bridge of his long nose. Possessing respect in oneself did not automatically win you the respect of others. A salutary lesson he had learned the hard way, and one he intended to rectify very soon.

It was, in fact, his next major project.

Vito Martinez, the hotel's Head of Security, came to stand beside him. 'She's gone back to her room,' he said. 'He's just arrived in the casino bar.'

'Tense?' Luiz asked.

'Yeah,' Vito replied, 'humming with it. Ripe, I'd say,'

he added, the evidence of his on-the-street New York up-bringing more pronounced in the dry-edged judgement.

A single nod in acknowledgement and Luiz Vazquez was turning away from the window, his expression, as always, a tightly closed book—not surprising for a man who'd used to play poker as lethally as he had.

'Buzz me when he comes to the tables,' was all he said. Then he was walking out of the control room, his long, lean level stride taking him across the elegant cream and black marbled floor of this tightly secured inner sanctum, then in through another door, which he closed behind him.

Silence suddenly prevailed.

Where the other room had been alive with a busy hum of activity, this room was so quiet you could hear a pin drop on the thick cream carpet covering its huge expanse. It was a luxuriously furnished room, plain but dramatic, with its modern black lacquered and leather furnishings enhanced by the simplicity of cream-painted walls.

Like the man himself, the room revealed nothing of his true personality. Except, maybe, for the black-framed picture hanging on the wall behind a large black-lacquered desk.

In its own way the picture was as dramatically plain as everything else in here—nothing more than the faint gold outline of a scorpion clinging to a white background with its lethal-looking tail curving upwards and over its scaly body in preparation to strike.

But it made the blood run cold just to look at it. For, although it was Luiz Vazquez's chair that was situated directly beneath that lethal claw, it was not him the scorpion seemed to threaten—but whoever was unlucky enough to sit in the chair placed on the other side of the desk.

Its message was clear. Mess with me and I strike.

It was his mark—his logo. Or one of them, at least. But

once upon a time the sign of the golden scorpion had used to adorn everything Luiz Vazquez was involved in. He had since learned to be much more subtle. And he just kept this one picture around him for personal reasons now—and as a warning to anyone who was unfortunate enough to find themselves summoned to these private rooms, that the cool-headed, soft-talking Luiz Vazquez still had a vicious sting in his tail.

But these days he was known better for his new logo. The one which gave his string of exclusive, internationally renowned hotels their name and had earned him quite a reputation for quality service and comfort during the last ten years.

For this was an Angel Hotel. Angel as in Luiz *Angeles* de Vazquez. Angel as in good, honest and true.

The sublime to the ridiculous. And an example of what good marketing could do because all of his hotels possessed in-house casinos which were the real draw. The luxury his admittedly well-heeled guests enjoyed while they played was just an added bonus.

The scorpion was probably a far more honest representation of what Luiz Vazquez really was.

Luiz went to sit beneath that scorpion now, sliding his perfectly contoured frame into a thickly padded swivel desk chair before reaching down to unlock and open one of the drawers in the desk.

His fingers, so long and lean and beautifully co-ordinated that they revealed even more about the man's extraordinary powers of self-control in the way they did everything with such neat precision, took out the only item in the drawer and placed it on the desktop.

It was a leather-bound dossier, expensive but nothing particularly ominous about it. Yet he didn't immediately open it. Instead he leant back in the chair and began swinging it lightly while one set of neatly filed fingernails tapped an absent tattoo against the desk. His expression revealed nothing, as usual. Whatever was going on in that shrewd, sharp mind of his was being kept hidden beneath the curling black lashes that usually shrouded his eyes.

Beautiful eyes. Eyes of a rich, dark fathomless brown colour that sat in the sleepy hollows of an arrestingly handsome face. A full Spaniard by birth, though raised in America, he undoubtedly had the warm golden skin of his Spanish forebears, the high cheekbones, the nose, the rock-solid, firmly chiselled jaw-line, and the shadowy outline of a beautifully moulded mouth.

But, for all of its good points, it was still the face of a cool operator. Of a man reputed to possess no heart—or, to be less fanciful, to possess the heart of an athlete, able to maintain the calm, steady pace necessary to keep the oxygen pumping into his clever brain no matter what pressure he put it under.

The fingers suddenly stopped tapping and moved, sliding over the desk and across smooth leather until they could curl and flick open the dossier cover to reveal a thick wad of documents stacked inside. With a supple dexterity that had been trained into his fingers years ago, he began sifting through the papers until he found the one he was looking for. Removing it from the stack, he set it neatly back down upon the top, then simply went still, his eyes glowing with a sudden burn as he sat there looking at a seven-by-nine colour photograph of—Caroline.

She was without doubt extraordinarily beautiful. No one with eyes would ever say she was not. Hair the colour of ripening wheat framed the most delicately perfect face even Luiz Vazquez, for all his thirty-five years of worldly experience, had ever set eyes upon. She had the flawless white skin of a pale English rose and eyes the colour of amethyst. Her small straight nose was classically drawn, like the finely defined curve of her delicate jaw-line. But it was her mouth that held Luiz's attention. Soft, warm, pink and full—it was a mouth made to drive a man wild with pleasure.

And he should know, Luiz mused cynically. For he'd had plenty of experience of just what that mouth could do—and he meant to have some more very soon.

It was a prospect that had the burn in his eyes changing back to their normal inscrutable cool as he utilised yet another facet of his strong character. Patience. The man was blessed with unending patience when it came to goals he had set himself.

That next goal was Caroline. And he was so sure of success that in his mind Caroline already belonged to him. It was this kind of belief in himself which gave him the power to put her photograph aside and basically forget it was there while he set about reading through the rest of the papers in the bulky dossier.

They were mostly bills. Final demand notes, warnings of foreclosure on bank loans, property mortgages, and, most sinister of all, the long list of unpaid gambling debts—both the old and the very new. He read each one in turn, consigning every detail to his photographic memory before setting it aside and doing the same with the next one.

A light on the desk console suddenly began flashing. Reaching out, he stabbed at the console with a finger. 'Yes?' he said.

'She's on her way down,' Vito Martinez informed him. 'He's playing for big money.'

'Right,' was all Luiz replied, and another stab at the console brought silence back to the room again.

Turning his attention back to the papers in front of him,

he picked them all up—including the photograph—deftly
re-stacked the pile, then shut the dossier and locked it away
in its drawer before getting smoothly to his feet. Then,
with a deft tug which brought white shirt-cuffs into line
with the edge of his creamy white dinner jacket, Luiz
Vazquez rounded his desk and strode out of the room.

Back in the control room, Vito Martinez was still standing by the window. Luiz went to join him, saw Vito's nod
and followed its direction to one of the roulette tables.

Tall, lean, quite good-looking for his age, and, as always, impeccably presented, Sir Edward Newbury was
playing big chips—and the expression on his face was a
mere hair's breadth away from fever-pitch.

Luiz recognised the look for exactly what it was—a man
in the last throes of civility. Sir Edward was hooked—
overdosing, in fact, and ready to sell his soul to the very
devil.

Ripe, as Vito had said.

Grimly unsurprised by what he was seeing, Luiz then
shifted his attention away from Sir Edward Newbury as,
with his usual faultless timing, he looked towards the casino entrance just as Caroline appeared.

And everything inside him went perfectly still.

Seven long years had gone by since he had last physi-
cally laid eyes on her—yet she had barely changed. The
hair, the eyes, the wonderful skin, the gorgeous mouth with
the vulnerable upper lip and cushion-soft lower one he
knew tasted as delicious as it looked. Even the long and
slender line of her figure, so perfectly outlined by the exquisite styling of her black dress, had not lost any of its
youthful firmness—as his own body was in the process of
informing him, growing hot around the loins in a way only
this woman had ever managed to kindle.

'His weakness', he labelled the sensation. The Spanish

bastard's desire to possess the forbidden in this woman, who was an icon to class and breeding. Even her name was something special. Miss Caroline Aurora Celandine Newbury... Luiz tasted the name on his silent tongue. She had a family tree that read like a history book, a background education fashioned exclusively for the élite, and a stately home any king would envy.

These were the credentials that gave the Newburys the right to consider themselves noble, Luiz judged cynically. To be good enough to be accepted by them you had to be someone at least as special. Even now, he predicted, when metaphorically they were down on their knees and could not afford to be too choosy, quality of breeding would be the yardstick by which they would measure whether or not you were worthy of their notice.

Caroline looked very pale, he saw as he watched her anxiously scanning the casino in search of her wayward father. She also looked tense and severely uncomfortable with her surroundings. But then she never had liked places like this.

She caught sight of Sir Edward as the roulette wheel began to spin. Luiz watched her body stiffen, watched the strain etch itself onto her lovely face and her small white teeth come pressing down into that exquisitely shaped bottom lip as she made herself walk forwards. He felt his own teeth set hard behind the flat line of his lips as he watched her pause a couple of steps behind her father, then knot her fingers together across the flatness of her stomach as if she wasn't quite sure just what to do next.

Really, what Caroline would have liked to do was get hold of her father by the scruff of his neck and drag him by it out of there. It was the breeding that stopped her; Luiz knew that. In the laws of polite society one did not make ugly scenes in public, no matter how bad the situation. Even when you knew that your finances were already in Queer Street and that what your father was doing was nothing short of criminal.

Black. Even. Sir Edward lost, as he had been doing steadily since they'd arrived here in Marbella late yesterday.

As the old man made a gesture of frustration, Caroline visibly wilted.

'Daddy...'

Luiz could actually feel her wariness as she placed a hand on the sleeve of her father's tux in an attempt to make him listen to reason.

No chance, Luiz judged. The man was half crazed with gambling fever. Once it hit there was no quick cure. Sir Edward could not give up now, even if he lost the very shirt from his back, and more.

It was the 'more' Luiz wanted.

After an initial start of surprise, then a guilty glance over his shoulder, Sir Edward Newbury turned petulant, and, with a tersely uttered sentence, shrugged off his daughter's hand so he could place another stack of chips on the table. All Caroline could do was stand and watch as five thousand pounds sterling hovered in the balance between a ball landing on black or on red.

Black. Sir Edward lost again.

Again Caroline attempted to stop him. Again her pleas were petulantly thrust aside. Only this time Luiz found his hands clenching into tight fists at his sides when he caught the briefest glint of telling moisture touching lovely eyes. It was sheer hopelessness that sent them on a hunting scan of the crowded casino, as if searching for help where none would ever be found.

Then, without any warning, she suddenly glanced up at the control room, those incredible eyes homing directly in

on him with such unerring accuracy that he caught his
breath.

So did Vito. 'Jeez,' he breathed.

Luiz did not so much as move a single muscle. He knew
she couldn't see him; he knew the glass did not allow her
to. Yet...

His skin began to prickle, a fine tremor of response rip-
pling through his whole body on a moment's complete loss
of himself as he stared straight into those beautiful, bright
tear-washed eyes. His throat had locked; his heart was
straining against a sudden fierce tightening across his
breastplate. Then her soft mouth gave a tremulous quiver
in a wretched display of absolute despair—and his whole
body was suddenly bathed in a fine layer of static elec-
tricity.

That mouth. That small, lush, sensual mouth—

'He won,' Vito murmured quietly beside him.

From the corner of his eye Luiz caught Sir Edward
Newbury's response as he punched the air with a trium-
phant fist. But his attention remained fixed on Caroline,
who was just standing there watching, with a dullness that
said winning was as bad as losing to her.

Abruptly he turned away. 'I'm going down,' he told
Vito. 'Make sure everything is ready for when we leave
here.'

And neither his voice nor his body language gave away
any hint of the burst of blistering emotion he had just been
put through before he strode away.

'Yes!' On a soft burst of exultation, Sir Edward
Newbury turned and scooped his daughter into his arms.
'Two wins on the trot! We've hit a winning streak, my
darling! A couple more like this and we'll be flying high!'

But he was already high. The wild glint burning in his

eyes was frightening. 'Please, Daddy,' Caroline pleaded. 'Stop now while you're ahead. This is—'

Madness, she had been going to say, but he brusquely cut her off. 'Don't be a killjoy, Caro. This is our lucky night, can't you see that?' Letting her go, he twisted back to the table as the croupier was about to slide his winnings over to him. 'Let them ride,' he instructed, and Caroline had to look on helplessly as every penny he had won was instantly waged on one feckless spin of a roulette wheel.

A crowd had started to gather around the table, their excited murmurs dying to a hush as the wheel began to spin. Caroline stopped breathing, her tongue cleaving to the roof of her paper-dry mouth as she watched that small ivory ball perform its tantalising dance with fate.

Inside she was angry—furious, even. But she had been reared never to make scenes in public. And the fact that he knew it was a weapon her father was more than happy to use against her. It was the nature of his weakness to rely on her good behaviour while he behaved appallingly.

So much for sincere promises, she derided as she watched through glazed eyes as the wheel began to slow. So much for weeks and months and *years* of careful vigilance, when she'd learned that trusting anything he said was a way to look disaster in the face.

She was tired of it, wearied with fighting the fight at the expense of everything else in her life. And she had a horrible feeling that this time she was not going to be able to forgive him for doing this to her yet again.

But for now all she could do was look on, feeling helpless, locked inside her own worst nightmare in the one place in this world her nightmares could be guaranteed free reign. This place, this hotel—this wretched casino. All she needed now was for Luiz Vazquez to materialise in front of her and the nightmare would be complete.

Like lightning striking twice. She shuddered.

Someone came to stand directly behind her, she felt their warm breath caressing her nape, though she only registered it vaguely. Her attention was fixed on that tormenting little ball and the rhythmic clacking noise it made as it jumped from compartment to compartment in a playful mix of ivory, red and black.

And the tension, the pulsing sense of building expectancy that was the real draw, the actual smell of madness, permeated all around her like a poisonous drug no one could resist.

'Yes!' Her father's victorious hiss hit her eardrums like the jarring clash of a hundred cymbals as he doubled his reckless stake—just like that.

The gathered crowd began enjoying his good fortune with him, but Caroline wilted like a dying flower. Her heart was floundering somewhere down deep inside her. She felt sick, she felt dizzy—must have actually swayed a little, because an arm snaked around her waist to support her. And it was a mark as to just how weak she was feeling that she let that arm gently ease her back against the hard-packed body standing behind her.

This was it, she was thinking dully. There would be no stopping him now. He wouldn't be happy until he had lost everything he had already won—and more. She didn't so much as consider him winning, because winning was not the real desire that drove people like him to play. It was, quite simply, the compulsion to play no matter what the final outcome. Winning meant your luck was in, so you played until your luck ran out, then played until it came back again.

A fine shudder rippled through her, making her suddenly aware that she was leaning against some total stranger. With an abrupt tensing of her spine, she managed to put a little distance between them before turning within that circling arm to murmur a coldly polite, 'Thank you, but I'm—'

Words froze, the air sealed inside lungs that suddenly ceased to function as she stood there, staring into a pair of all too familiar devil-black eyes that trapped her inside a world of complete denial.

'Hello, Caroline,' Luiz greeted smoothly.

CHAPTER TWO

HER heart flipped over, then began to beat wildly. 'Luiz...' she breathed through lips gone too numb to move while, No, her mind was telling her. She was hallucinating—dreaming him up from the depths of her worst fears—because this place and her father's madness were all so synonymous in her mind with this man. 'No.' She even made the denial out loud.

'Sorry but—yes,' he replied with a real dry amusement slicing through his lazy tone.

But it was an amusement that did not reach the darkness in his eyes, and the room began to blacken around its edges as yet another dizzying sense of pained dismay took the place of shocked numbness.

'Please let go of me,' she said shakily, desperately needing to put some distance between the two of them before she could attempt to deal with this.

'Of course.' The hand was instantly removed. And for some crazy reason she found herself comparing his ready compliance with the complete disregard the stranger in the basement had shown when she had made the same request of him.

A man who had reminded her of Luiz. A man she hadn't liked on sight, whereas Luiz she...

'Your father's luck is in, I see,' he remarked, his gaze now fixed on what was going on behind her.

'Is it?' Scepticism sliced heavily through the two short syllables, bringing his dark eyes back to her face.

But Caroline could no longer look at him. It *hurt* to look at him. For Luiz personified everything she had learned to

26

despise about her father's disease. Obsession, machination, deception, betrayal.

Bitterness suddenly rose to almost completely engulf her. She went to spin away from him, but at the same moment the crowd began to surge in, jostling her in their eagerness to congratulate her father, wanting to demonstrate their delight in seeing someone beat the bank against all the odds for once. Luiz's arm came back, looping round her in protection this time against several elbows being aimed in her direction, and Caroline found herself being pressed so close to him that she would have to be dead not to be aware of every hard-packed nuance of the man.

Her heart-rate picked up and her breathing grew shallow. It was awful. Memories began to flood her mind. They had been lovers once. Their bodies knew each other as intimately as two bodies could. Standing here, virtually imprisoned by the crowd closing round them, was the worst kind of punishment that fate could have doled out to her for being stupid enough to agree to come back here.

It was a knowledge that filled her with a kind of acrimony that poured itself into her voice. 'Still playing games for a living, Luiz?' she shot at him sarcastically. 'I wonder what the management would do if they found out they have a professional in their club.'

His dark eyes narrowed. And it was because she was being forced to stand so close to him that she felt the slight tensing of certain muscles—like a dangerous cat raising its hackles. 'Was that your version of a veiled threat by any chance?' he questioned very carefully.

Was it? Caroline asked herself, aware that all it would take was a quiet word in the ear of the management to have Luiz very quietly but very firmly hustled out of here. But—

'It was merely an observation,' she sighed, knowing that

she had no right to criticise Luiz when her own father was just as bad.

'Then, to answer your *observation,* no,' he replied. 'I am not here to play.'

But Caroline wasn't listening. A sudden idea had hit her, one that had her heart leaping in her breast. 'Luiz…' she murmured urgently. 'If I had a quiet word with the management about my father, would they stop *him* from playing any more?'

'Why should they?' His mouth took on a derisive twist. 'He's no professional, just a man with a vice he has turned into an obsession.'

'A suicidal obsession,' Caroline extended with a shiver.

The hand at her spine gently soothed her. And what was worse was that Luiz didn't say a single word. He knew her father—knew him only too well.

'I hate this,' she whispered, wishing she could just creep away and pretend it wasn't happening. But she couldn't, and somehow, some way she had to try and stop this madness before her father ruined them completely.

'Do you want me to stop him?' Luiz offered.

Her eyes flicked up to clash with his. 'Do you think you can?' she murmured anxiously.

In response Luiz simply lifted his gaze to where her father was emerging from his sea of congratulations. 'Sir Edward,' he said.

That was all. No raising of his voice, no challenge in the tone. Just the two quietly spoken words. Yet they carried enough impact to cause a small cessation in the buzz of excitement taking place.

And the fine hairs on the back of Caroline's neck began to tingle as she sensed her father spinning around. She couldn't see him because Luiz was keeping her pressed against him, but in the following long seconds of tense silence she certainly felt the full thrust of her father's shock.

His recovery was swift though. 'Well,' he drawled. 'If it isn't Luiz. This is a surprise...'

Eton-educated, brought up to be always aware of his own worth, Sir Edward Newbury's King's-English accent was a pitch-perfect blend of sarcasm and condescension that made his daughter wince.

Luiz didn't wince. He just offered a wry smile. 'Isn't it?' he agreed. 'Seven years on and here we are again. Same time, same place—'

'It must be fate,' her father dryly tagged on.

And fate just about covered it, Caroline was thinking hollowly. Ill fate. Cruel fate.

'I see your luck is in tonight,' Luiz observed. 'Taken the bank to the cleaners, have you?'

'Not yet, but I'm getting there.' Her father sounded different suddenly. Enlivened, invigorated.

At which point Caroline made herself turn in the circle of Luiz's arm to witness for herself the covetous gleam she knew was going to be in her father's eyes. But she also saw the childlike pique that took hold of him as he skimmed his gaze over her face. He knew very well how badly he was letting her down tonight, but was belligerently defiant about it.

It made her heart want to break in despair.

'How much do you think you've managed to win so far?' Luiz questioned curiously.

Sir Edward didn't even give his winnings a glance. 'Bad luck to count it, Luiz. You know that,' he dismissed with a shrug.

'But if you're feeling really lucky, then perhaps you could be tempted into a private bet with me?' Luiz suggested. 'Put the lot on the next spin,' he challenged. 'If you win, I'll double the amount, then play you for the lot at poker. Fancy the long shot?' he added provokingly, ignoring Caroline's protesting gasp.

Their curious audience was suddenly on edge. Caroline simply went cold. Luiz called this *stopping him?* In all her life she had never felt so betrayed—and that included the last time Luiz had betrayed her trust in him.

'No,' she whispered, her eyes pleading with her father not to take Luiz on.

But he wasn't even aware of her presence any more. And she knew exactly what he was doing; he was busily adding up his present winnings, doubling them and doubling them again, then playing Luiz at a game even she knew Luiz was lethal at, and seeing all his problems melting away in one sweet lucky night.

'Why not?' He accepted the challenge, and as his daughter stared at him in dismay he turned and, with a brief nod of his head to the waiting croupier, coolly instructed, 'Let it all ride.'

And the wheel began to spin once again.

Behind her Caroline could feel Luiz watching things over the top of her head. In front of her, her father stood, outwardly calm and supremely indifferent to the eventual outcome even though their lives, in effect, stood hovering in the balance. And all around it was as if the whole casino had come to a breathless standstill while everyone watched the game play itself out. There wasn't a person present who believed that Sir Edward could win on the same colour for a fourth time.

Caroline certainly did not believe it. 'I'll never forgive you for this,' she told Luiz, and shrugged herself free of his grasp.

He let her go, though he remained standing directly behind her. And, like everyone else, they stood watching as the wheel began to slow, allowing that wretched ball to bounce playfully from slot to slot.

It was torture at its worst. She had known they should not have come here, had told her father over and over again that Marbella was the last place on earth they should look for salvation.

But he hadn't listened. He was desperate, and desperate men do desperate things. 'We have no choice!' was all he'd said. 'The finance company that bought up all our debts is based in Marbella. They refuse to speak to us unless we show up personally. We have to go there, Caroline.'

'And your gambling debts?' she'd hit out at him angrily. 'Do they have their greedy hands on all of those too?'

He'd flushed with guilt, then gone peevish on her as he always did when caught by his own inadequacies. 'Do you want to help sort this mess out or not?' he'd challenged harshly.

She had, but not this way. Not by banking everything they had on the spin of a stupid roulette wheel.

The dizziness returned, the blood seeping slowly out of her head as if squeezed by that steadily slowing wheel. Then, quite suddenly, it stopped. Silence hit the room. No one moved for the space of a few tense breathless seconds—until Sir Edward said, very calmly, 'Mine, I think.'

Without uttering a single word, Caroline turned and walked away, leaving the melee to erupt behind her.

How much had he won? She didn't know. When would he play Luiz? She didn't care. As far as she was concerned the whole miserable thing was well and truly over. She'd had enough—more than enough—and she never wanted to step foot in a place like this again.

She even felt a real disgust with herself for being talked into coming here at all. She should have known he couldn't keep his word. Should have known he didn't really care what happened to them so long as he could get his kicks.

The casino doors swung shut behind her. Eyes bright, mouth tight, body stiff with tension, she walked towards the stairwell with the intention of going back to their room. But suddenly she knew she couldn't do that, couldn't just go back there and await the next instalment in her father's quest for utter ruin. And on an impulse she didn't think to question, she found her feet were taking her across the basement foyer and towards the pair of doors that stood opposite the casino.

She'd half expected the swimming pool room to be locked at this time of the night but it wasn't, she discovered, though the lights had been turned down to their minimum, so only the pool itself was illuminated, showing glass-smooth cool blue water—and not another person in sight.

Without really considering her next actions, Caroline stepped out of her shoes, unzipped her dress and draped it over the back of a nearby chair, then simply dived cleanly into the water.

Why she did it, she didn't know, and cared even less that she had dived in wearing bra, panties and even her black stockings and suspenders. She just powered up and down that pool like someone intent on winning a medal.

She was performing her fourth lap when she noticed Luiz sitting in the chair next to the one on which she had placed her dress. The cold cut of her eyes completely blanked him as she made a neat rolling turn then headed back down the pool.

He was still there when she made her sixth cutting crawl through the water, still sitting there on her eighth. By the tenth her lungs were beginning to burst and she had to pause for breath. Crossing her arms on the tiled rim, she rested her brow against them and stayed like that until the panting began to ease.

'Feel better for that?' Luiz questioned levelly.

'No,' she replied, and at last lifted her face to look at him. 'Do you, for playing the voyeur?'

'You are wearing more than most women do who use this pool,' he casually pointed out.

'But a gentleman, on noting the difference, would have had the grace to leave.'

'And we both know that I am no gentleman,' he smilingly tagged on as if on cue.

Had she been cueing him to admit that? Caroline asked herself. Yes, she accepted, she had. It pleased her, for some reason, to make Luiz admit to what he was.

Or wasn't, she amended. 'Where's my father?'

'Counting his winnings, I should imagine.' His shrug demonstrated his complete indifference. 'Are you ready to get out of there?' he enquired then. 'Or are you expecting me to strip off and join you?'

'I'm coming out,' she decided immediately, not even considering whether or not his suggestion was a bluff. Past experience of this man's dangerous streak made her sure that he was quite capable of stripping to the skin then joining her without hesitation.

And she had no wish whatsoever to see Luiz Vazquez strip. Didn't need to, to know exactly what he looked like naked. Just as he didn't need to see her remove the black silk bra, stockings and panties to know exactly what was hiding beneath, she added grimly as, with another neat roll, she took herself underwater to swim to the nearest set of steps.

By the time she rose up again Luiz was standing at the edge, waiting with a large white towel stretched out at the ready. Where he had got it from Caroline didn't know, and found that once again she didn't really care. It was as if her brain had gone on strike where caring was concerned.

So she climbed up the steps and calmly took the towel

from him with a 'Thank you' murmured politely, and no hint of anything else in her tone.

He noticed the absence of emotions, of course. 'You're being very calm about this,' he remarked.

Caroline wrapped the towel sarong-wise around her body. 'I hate and despise you. Will that do?' she offered, bending to squeeze the excess water out of her hair.

He grimaced. 'It's a start. Do you want me to get another towel to dry your hair with?'

Finger-combing the wet tangles, she tossed back her head to send the chin-length bob flying back from her face. The swim had seen off most of her make-up other than her mascara, which now stood out sooty black in a naturally porcelain-white face.

'I want nothing from you, Luiz,' she told him. 'Because your idea of a favour is to cut off the outstretched hand.'

'Ah...' His own hands slid smoothly into the pockets of his black silk evening trousers. 'The hand I cut off, I have to presume, belonged to you?'

She didn't want to talk about it, so she turned away. Spying her dress on the chair, she went to pick it up. 'I'm going to my room,' she announced, walking towards the pool house door. 'Goodbye, Luiz,' she added coldly. 'I would like to say that it was nice to see you again, but I would be lying, so I won't bother...'

It would have been the perfect exit line too, if Luiz hadn't spoiled it. 'Haven't you forgotten something?' he prompted lazily.

She stopped, turned, and frowned at him in puzzlement. He was still standing more or less where she had left him, tall, lean, superbly presented against a backcloth of shimmering blue, and sexily dark and disturbing enough to make any girl's heart squeeze.

Caroline's heart gave that terrible little squeeze. And she

despised herself for being so susceptible to him, knowing him for what he was.

'Your purse and your shoes,' he kindly pointed out to her, and went to collect them from where she had left them, the purse thrown down on the chair, the shoes kicked carelessly beneath.

The shoes he casually held out towards her, dangling them from their straps on long lean fingers. Tight-lipped she took them, but when she went to reach for her purse Luiz slid it smoothly into one of his cream tux pockets.

'Give it back to me, please,' she commanded.

But he just offered her a lazy smile. 'With that prim tone you could be my headmistress,' he mocked.

'How would you know?' she hit back. 'The way I remember you telling it, you rarely bothered to attend school.'

His soft laugh was appreciative, but his tone held something else entirely when he added, 'Oh, I've known a few stiff-backed, cold-eyed females in my time.'

Which instantly reminded her of all the state institutes he had lived in during his childhood. And her inner eye was suddenly seeing a dark-haired, dark-eyed, lonely little Spanish boy who, even at the tender age of nine, had known exactly what it was like to rely only on himself for survival.

How many confidences had they exchanged during that long hot summer seven years ago? she wondered as a disturbing little ache took up residence in her stomach.

And how much of what he'd told her had been the truth? she then added cynically. And how much merely words calculated to earn her soft-hearted sympathy—while he quietly and calculatedly fleeced her father across a green baize table?

'What's the grimace for?'

Huskily intimate, disturbingly close. She blinked,

glanced up, found he had shifted his stance slightly and now had a shoulder leaning against the crack between the two doors. It was such an obvious blocking tactic that Caroline was instantly on her guard.

'My bag please, Luiz,' she insisted, ignoring his question to hold out the hand from which her shoes now dangled from her own slender fingers.

He in turn ignored both the command and the outstretched hand. 'Did you know that your eyes go grey when you're angry?' he murmured.

Messages began to sting through her blood. Sexual messages. 'My bag,' she repeated.

He sent her a spine-tingling smile. 'And your mouth goes all prim and—'

'Stop it,' she snapped. 'This is childish!'

'Exciting...' he argued.

She heaved out a breath that was supposed to relay irritation but only managed to sound fraught. And her outstretched fingers began to tremble, so she closed them into a fist and returned them to what they had been doing, which was keeping her towel in place.

'I'm beginning to catch cold standing around here like this!'

And sure enough she started to shiver, though whether from cold or from something else entirely she refused to let herself consider. But, whatever the reason, it diverted Luiz away from his lazy teasing. And, with a swiftness that completely threw her, he straightened from the door to whip off his jacket then settle it around her wet shoulders.

The oddly gallant gesture sent her defences crumbling. Tears flooded into her eyes. 'Don't play him, Luiz,' she pleaded huskily.

'Here,' he prompted, taking her dress and shoes from

her fingers. 'Feed your arms into the sleeves then get rid of that wet towel...'

It was a refusal to listen in anyone's books. Despair wriggled through her while she obeyed him without thinking and pushed her arms into the sleeves of his jacket. The silk lining was warm against her cool damp skin, the scent of him suddenly swirling all around her.

'I thought you were going to help me,' she choked. 'But all you've done is make matters worse!'

'Madness only responds to the prospect of more madness,' he answered quietly. 'The only way to stop him tonight was by giving him a good reason to stop. So we play in an hour, away from the hotel, because I am not—'

His words were cut off mid-flow when Caroline reached up to press both hands to his shirt-front in pained appeal. 'Please don't do it! How can you want to do this to me all over again?'

But Luiz wasn't listening. Instead he was staring down at the place where her hands lay spread across the fine white linen covering his breastbone. His own hands came up to cover hers, and suddenly she was made acutely aware of hot flesh, of the prickly evidence of very male body hair, of the hard pack of muscle and the solid thump of a living heart beating steadily beneath it all.

A heart she knew could rage out of control when he was in the throes of passion. A silk-fleshed body she could remember moving against her own. And that thick crisp mat of chest hair sweeping down like an arrow, aimed directly at his—

Her mouth ran dry. The sex was back. That burning, pulsing, nagging ache that was tugging her senses into life. His hands moved, leaving her hands so he could slide his fingers beneath his jacket, and the towel suddenly slid to the floor. Skin touched skin. Caroline arched on a gasping response.

'No,' she groaned when she dared to let her eyes make contact with the burn now taking place at the back of his.

Luiz didn't answer. It was too late anyway, because he'd closed the gap and was kissing her—kissing her like a lover—fiercely, deeply, and so very intimately that she was utterly shattered by how beautiful it was.

I've missed him, she thought, and felt the tears return. I've missed the power with which we affect each other, the passion we can generate with just a simple touch. Her fingers moved, drifting up his shirt and to his face, where they traced each contour with the fever of a blind woman Braille-reading her most treasured possession.

He responded with a sigh that shivered through both of them, and he brought her into even closer contact with him, close enough for her senses to fly when she felt the throbbing evidence of his pleasure.

And she knew it was crazy, but in these few brief sensual moments, she knew that Luiz belonged to her. She owned him. She *possessed* him. If she said, Die for me, Luiz, he would die.

But, more than that, as incredible as that might seem, she would also die for him.

'Luiz...' she breathed into his mouth.

The soft breathy sound had the most powerful effect on him. On a low growl, he literally submerged her in a hot and hungry flood of heat that completely consumed her will to fight.

If she'd ever had any, she derided herself. Luiz was her weakness, just as gambling was her father's. Once you acquired an addiction it remained with you for life. Starve it for years and it would still erupt at the first tiny, tempting sip. And she was certainly sipping at her addiction, she admitted as she fell into the kiss with all the urgency of starvation, tasting him, touching him, needing him, wanting more!

His hands caressed her and she let them, his mouth devoured hers and she allowed it to. She could taste mint on his breath and on the moistness of his tongue, and feel the deep throb of his heart beneath her restless fingers.

Something gave between them. She hardly understood what it was until her breasts were swinging free and Luiz's hands were taking possession. After that the whole thing became a banquet at its most ravenous. He deserted her mouth to go in search of other delights, and she tossed back her head and simply preened with pleasure while he licked and sucked and teased her breasts.

It felt perfectly natural to lift up one long silken leg and hook it around his lean waist for balance as she arched to offer him easier access. But the action brought her into even more intimate contact with the hard masculine core of him. And after that she became lost in a burning bright kaleidoscope filled with touch and feel and sound and scents that were so entrenched in her psyche because this man had been her first lover. The one who'd taught her to feel like this, to respond like this, to need like this!

Her *only* lover—though she hoped to goodness that Luiz couldn't tell that was the case. Couldn't tell that she was responding this wildly and this helplessly because he was the only man ever to make her feel like this.

And while it happened it didn't seem to matter that he was also the man who'd completely shattered her once, betrayed her so badly that she had never been able to recover. Her father didn't matter. The game didn't matter. The knowledge that Luiz could only hurt her again didn't matter.

In fact she was so lost in what he was doing to her that when the knock sounded on the pool room door she could barely comprehend what the sound meant. Until Luiz straightened abruptly, thrust her leg away, then clamped her weak and trembling frame to his own pulsing body before reaching out to open the door a crack.

At which point the shock waves of what they had been so close to actually doing, began ricocheting horribly through her system. Seven years with no contact, she was thinking dizzily, and they'd fallen on each other like a pair of hungry animals at the first opportunity they had been handed.

It was all so utterly, shamefully vulgar that she buried her burning face in Luiz's throat and hoped to God that the person knocking on the door was not her father.

A man's voice she had never heard before, but which had the same American drawl as Luiz, said, 'It's all arranged. You have half an hour.'

'Okay,' Luiz acknowledged gruffly, quickly shut the door again, then with a firmness that utterly shook her, he put her from him.

It took her a few moments to realise what was happening, but one glance at his coldly closed face and she knew that the passionately out-of-control man she had been kissing had suddenly turned back into her enemy.

'What's arranged?' she asked tautly.

'What do you think?' he replied.

He meant his game with her father, she realised. Even after what had just erupted between them he was still going to play him.

'Here…' Bending down, he picked up her dress where it had fallen to the floor at some unknown point. 'Put this on; you're dry enough. We have things to do and you can't leave here looking like this.'

Looking like this… Through glazed eyes Caroline stared down at herself, saw the pulsing tightness of her distended nipples, her flushed skin, her long white thighs still trembling from the way he had made her feel. Even Luiz's jacket was no longer where she'd thought it was.

He was shrugging it back onto his own broad shoulders with what was a callous disregard for her raw sensibilities as she stood there almost naked in front of him, feeling completely humiliated and cheap.

Instead of burning up with undiluted passion she was now icy cold with dismay. The nausea arrived, attacking her throat and forcing her to swallow thickly a couple of times before she dared let herself speak.

'I hate you,' she whispered.

'Not as much as you would like to, I think,' was his reply.

She was completely demolished by it, because it was such a dreadful truth. Slipping back into her dress took the concentrated effort of just about every brain cell that hadn't been atomised. As she shimmied the black crêpe up her body, she noticed her bra lying on the tiled floor and wanted to crawl away in shame.

Luiz bent to scoop it up, stuffing the flimsy piece of silk into one of his pockets before turning her around to do up her zip. She moved like a rag doll, unable to think, unable to speak, and just stood there while he bent to feed her feet into her strappy black shoes.

He straightened again, then waited while her shaky fingers attempted to smooth some of the creases out of her dress. And the tension sizzling between them was dreadful. Not once did either attempt full eye contact. Not once did either of them attempt to speak again after that last telling comment of his.

When she eventually went still, in an indication that she had made the best of herself she could under the circumstances, Luiz opened the door, then stood back in a grim gesture for her to precede him back into the basement foyer.

The stranger she had encountered in the lift was standing talking to one of the dinner-suited bouncers. He glanced up as they appeared and was suddenly riveted. Caroline didn't even notice him; she was too busy being repulsed by the feel of Luiz's hand resting on her back as he escorted her to the stairwell.

She didn't want him to touch her now. She didn't want Luiz anywhere near her. Her chin was up, her head held high and her body erect—but her eyes were blind and inside she felt as if she were dying.

The moment they reached the upper main foyer, she stepped right away from him.

'Where are you going?'

Already two blissful steps away, Caroline paused but didn't turn. 'If you want to ruin my father a second time then go ahead,' she invited coldly. 'I certainly can't stop you—but I don't have to watch you.'

After that, she began walking again.

'But we haven't finished.' His hand came out to capture one of hers. And without another word he began trailing her across the foyer towards a door marked 'Private' that seemed to open magically as they approached it.

Frowning, because she just didn't understand what was happening here, she found herself inside yet another foyer that had her high heels tapping on black and cream marble. Luiz led her across to another door, which he opened by hand this time, gestured her to precede himself inside, then quietly closed the door behind them.

It was an office, Caroline saw. A very elegant black and cream office.

'What is this place?' she asked warily.

Stepping past her, Luiz walked across the room towards the desk, then placed himself behind it. 'My office,' he answered, bending down to unlock and open a drawer.

'You mean...' Her eyes flickered around the room. 'You mean, *you* actually *work* here?'

'Work here. Live here...' He placed a heavy leather-bound dossier on the desk in front of him. 'This is *my* hotel, Caroline,' he added levelly.

CHAPTER THREE

HIS hotel…? Caroline gave a small shake of her head. 'But this is an *Angel* Hotel,' she stated. 'Part of the *Angel* Group!' And the Angel Group was huge. Not just because of the string of deluxe hotels it owned throughout the world, but because it had other, much more powerful interests wrapped up in its multinational package.

Lifting his dark head, Luiz just looked at her. It was all it needed for the penny to drop. *Angel* as in Luiz *Angeles* de Vazquez, she was suddenly remembering. But it was the *Angel* in the Angel Group that was slowly filling Caroline with a new sense of dismay. Because it was also the group which had very recently acquired a bank in London that the Newbury family knew very well.

'Oh, my God,' she breathed, as full enlightenment finally began to dawn. 'It's you we have been summoned here to Marbella to see about our debts, isn't it?'

He didn't answer. But then he didn't really need to when confirmation was already written on his lean dark face. And she could only stand and watch as every image she had ever built in her mind to form Luiz Vazquez slowly cracked, then shattered right there in front of her until she could no longer see Luiz the exciting lover. Or even Luiz the ruthless con-man who'd fleeced her father of tens of thousands of pounds.

'What is it you want?' she whispered fraily as the shattered pieces that had once been Luiz settled back into their new order of things. And now she was seeing Luiz the ice-cool operator, whom, it seemed, had only gone up and up

43

in the world while she and her father had gone steadily down.

'I want you to come and sit down,' he said. 'We haven't got much time. And now that you understand just why you are here we may as well get down to business...'

Business. The word sent an icy chill chasing down her spine. As she walked across the room towards him on legs that were shaking badly Luiz sat himself down, opened the dossier, selected a piece of paper from it, then slid it towards her as she sank into the chair placed opposite him.

'Tell me if you agree with what's written on there,' he invited.

Eyes flickering in an effort to get them to focus, heart slowed by the weight of what was unfolding in front of her now, Caroline pulled the piece of paper towards her, then picked it up in trembling fingers and forced herself to read.

Finely listed, tightly lined, it was a very precise inventory of every penny she already knew they owed—and a whole lot more that she actually hadn't known about, but she couldn't doubt their authenticity when the names of all her father's favourite London haunts were inscribed next to them.

And the bottom figure was so utterly repellent that her skin began to crawl. 'Could I have some water, please?' she breathed.

Without a single word, Luiz got up and walked over to a black-lacquered sideboard. He returned in seconds to place a frosted glass of iced water down in front of her, then just as silently returned to his chair while she picked up the water and sipped at it sparingly.

'We can't pay you, Luiz,' she told him, once she'd found enough voice to speak. 'N-not all of it anyway.'

'I know that,' he returned.

She swallowed thickly, and took a couple more sips of

water before making herself go on. 'If you refuse to play him at cards tonight, then the money he won in the casino plus some money I have of my own should clear a small part of this.' But not all, she added with a silent bleakness. Not anywhere near all...

'The planned card game and this are two separate issues,' he informed her. 'And I never—ever—mix business with pleasure, Caroline. Understand me?'

Understand? No she didn't! 'But we have the means to clear s-some of this, Luiz!' she cried, tossing the wretched debt list back at him. 'And you want to play card games just for the hell of it? Where is the business sense in that?'

Sitting back in his chair, Luiz didn't even deign to watch as the piece of paper skidded across the table then floated down onto his lap. His face was inscrutable, his manner relaxed. 'Where is your own block of money coming from?' Smooth as silk, he kept the discussion fixed to his own agenda.

Her breath shuddered on an overwrought sigh. 'None of your business,' she muttered, then got up and paced tensely away from the desk.

'It is if you borrowed from Peter to pay back Paul, so to speak,' he pointed out. 'Which would only make the bottom figure here worse, not better.'

'I have money left over from my mother's bequest,' she told him reluctantly.

'No you don't.'

'What——?' Stung by his quiet certainty she spun to stare at him.

Instantly she felt under attack. It was his eyes, and the knowledge of truth she could see written in them.

'Your mother's money went on paying back debts years ago,' he informed her. 'After that you spent the next few years selling off the family heirlooms one by one, until there were very few left worth selling. Then came the quiet period when your father behaved himself for a couple of years—or so you believed. When it all started up again, you resorted to selling off small plots of land on the far edges of your family estate to wealthy businessmen who were looking for somewhere to build a country retreat. But the council eventually put a stop to that, quoting the rape of country heritage law or some such thing.

'So what's left to sell, Caroline?' he asked. 'The ancestral home, which is already mortgaged to the hilt? Or the few heirlooms that are left—which probably belong to the bank already, on paper at least? Or maybe you were thinking of paying me back with the commission you earn working for those London-based interior designers who pay you peanuts for your considerable knowledge of all things aesthetic, to hunt out pieces of artwork and various *objets d'art* to decorate the homes of their wealthy clients?'

It was like being pummelled into the ground by a very large mallet. She had never felt so small in her whole life.

'What next, Caroline?' He pummelled her some more with the soft pound of his ruthless voice. 'What could you possibly have left that would appease any bank holding a debt the size of yours? Yourself, maybe?' he suggested silkily. 'Are you thinking of prostituting yourself to the highest bidder so that Daddy can keep on feeding his addiction because he can't help himself?'

'Stop it!' she choked. 'Just shut up—*shut up!*' She couldn't listen to any more! White-faced, totally demolished, she stared at him in blank incomprehension as to why he was being so cruel. 'How do you know all of this? Where did you get your information? How long have you been compiling that—' she waved a shaky hand at the thick wad of paper sitting on the desk in front of him '—dossier on me?'

'Information can be bought any time, anywhere, so long as you have the money to pay for it.'

'And that makes it all right to pry into my life?' she cried. 'Why, Luiz—*why?*' She just didn't understand it! 'What did I ever do to you to make you want to pursue me in this h-horrible way? It was you that once used me, remember!' she added painfully. 'You slaked one of your lusts with my body, night after wretched night, then went off to slake your other lust at a card table with my father!'

'I don't want to talk about that,' he gritted, and he was suddenly on his feet. Tense—like her. Angry—like her. As bitter as hell—like her.

'Oh, that's rich!' Caroline scorned him. 'When it comes to *your* faults, *you* don't want to talk about it! Yet you've just taken great delight in listing *my* faults and failings— and even had the gall to call me a prostitute!'

'I made it an option, not a fact,' he corrected. But he looked pale—pale enough for Caroline to know that she had touched a raw nerve somewhere inside his ruthless soul.

'And we both know who sold himself for the pot of gold, Luiz,' Caroline persisted angrily. 'We both know that your motive for keeping me in bed with you was so I couldn't be keeping an eye on my father!'

'All right, let's have that one out,' he decided, swinging round the desk to begin striding towards her.

Caroline wanted to back off, but hell could freeze over before she would let herself do so. He arrived, big and threatening, right in front of her.

'You think I prostituted myself for the pot of gold seven years ago.' She *had* hit a raw nerve, Caroline confirmed. 'So let's just see which one of us can delve the depths this time. Here's the deal, Caroline. Take it or leave it,' he announced. 'Sleep with me tonight and I won't play your father.'

Sleep with him? He was lucky she didn't wing her hand at his face! 'Well, if that isn't mixing business with pleasure—what is?' she spat at him in disgust.

'No—no,' Luiz argued. 'This is called mixing pleasure with pleasure.' And he was even smiling, the black-hearted devil.

'Go to hell,' she told him, then spun on her heel with the intention of walking out of there as fast as she damn well could.

'The offer holds only as long as it takes you to open that door,' Luiz fed swiftly after her.

Her footsteps stilled, though her heart-rate didn't, it raged on right out of that door and onto the next flight out of this awful place! She converted that rage into a different kind of action by wheeling back round to face him. Luiz didn't need words to know what she was thinking. And his answering shrug spoke for itself.

'Everyone has a price, Caroline,' he taunted silkily. 'I am just trying to ascertain your price, that's all...'

'I'll never forgive you for this,' she breathed.

'By that, are you trying to tell me that it would *hurt* you to go to bed with me?' he questioned smoothly.

From feeling chilled she went hot—hot with discomfort. Because, after what they had just almost done in the pool room, there was no way she could pretend that sleeping with Luiz would be anything but a whole lot of pleasure!

A light suddenly began winking on the desk console, saving Caroline from having to make the worst decision of her entire life.

Luiz swung back to his desk, sat down in his chair again, then reached out to flick a finger at a switch. 'Yes?' he prompted.

'It's time we were leaving,' the same deep voice Caroline had first heard through the narrow gap in the pool room door informed him.

His eyes narrowed thoughtfully on Caroline. Quite unexpectedly she began to shake so badly that she just had to sit down. The chair she had just vacated was nearest. Almost stumbling over to it, she lowered herself down as Luiz murmured a quiet, 'Two minutes, Vito...' and cut the connection.

Too long spent riding a roller coaster of too many shocks and worries had shaken her insides to pieces. She stared helplessly at Luiz, and knew he was waiting for her to voice her surrender to him out loud.

On a sharp stab of pain she flicked her eyes away, because she couldn't bear to look at him *and* give him that surrender.

It was then that she saw it. 'Oh, good grief,' she gasped. She had only just noticed the scorpion crawling down the wall behind him. The picture was so life-like that she actually reared back in the chair to take instinctive avoiding action. 'Luiz—that thing is hideous!'

'But effective,' he smiled.

It was then she remembered that the first business he had ever owned outright had been a small nightclub in New York called, as he had informed her rather deridingly, The Scorpion, and bought from an old friend whose deteriorating health had forced him to accept a quieter way of life. Within two years Luiz had sold the club on to a big inner-city developer for the kind of money that had allowed him to give his own life new direction. 'And I haven't needed to look back since,' she recalled him saying to her with quiet satisfaction.

But the scorpion itself must still linger on in his affections for him to have it hanging there on his wall. Or was there more to its being there than mere affection? Was it a warning that this lean, dark, smoothly sophisticated man had another side to him that was as lethal as the scorpion's tail?

Glancing back at him, she found him watching her with the kind of mocking twist to his mouth that said he knew what she was thinking and was wryly amused by it.

'A scorpion stings its victims quick and clean, Luiz,' she murmured unsteadily. 'What you are proposing here is neither clean nor quick.'

'Unparalleled sex between two people who excite the hell out of each other? I should hope not.' He smiled, picking up the dossier to replace it in its drawer.

Then he was suddenly on his feet. 'Right,' he said briskly. 'Let's go...'

Let's go? Caroline's skin began to prickle as a fresh burst of alarm went chasing through her. 'But I haven't agreed to do anything with you yet!' she protested.

'Decide later,' he said as he came striding round the desk towards her. 'We haven't got time to deal with it right now.'

With that, Caroline found herself being lifted firmly to her feet. Her options, she realised, had dwindled to nothing. Time had seemingly run out. Without another word, Luiz was escorting her from the room and they were outside in the silky warm darkness before she realised what they were doing.

A top-of-the-range black BMW stood purring at the front entrance. Luiz opened the rear door and urged her inside before going round to climb in on the other side of the car. The moment the door shut the car was moving, driven by a man who was hidden behind a shield of smoked glass.

'Where are we going?'

'You'll see,' was the very uninformative reply she received.

It was late, but outside, beyond the car's side window, the resort was still alive with people out to enjoy themselves with a visit to one of Marbella's elegant night-spots or just simply taking a late stroll along the yacht-lined waterfront.

It was years since she'd been able to do what they were doing, since she'd felt carefree enough to want to.

Years and years of self-restraint, of living under a thick grey cloud with no hint of a silver lining. Years playing watchdog to her father's sickness, because she knew that if she didn't look out for him then nobody else was going to do it.

'He's fine,' Luiz murmured huskily beside her, reading her mind as if it already belonged to him. 'Stop worrying about him.'

Caroline heaved out a soft deriding laugh at the remark. For when had she *not* worried about her father? He had been a good old-fashioned rake in his heyday, and marriage hadn't really changed him. Though she thought— *hoped* that he had at least remained faithful to her mother.

No, she told herself firmly. Her father had been no philanderer. A rogue and a gambler, yes, but he'd loved her mother. If anything, all his old weaknesses had only re-emerged after her mother had died and he'd missed her so badly that he'd had to look for forgetfulness somewhere.

Or at least that was how it had been in the beginning. Now…? Her eyes glassed over, blocking out the need to look for the answer to that question because she already knew it.

The car began to climb out of the bay and into private villa country. Caroline recognised the area because she'd used to know so many people who owned holiday homes here. This had been her playground, a place for fun and carefree vacations away from the restrictions of boarding school during the long summer breaks. She'd used to have as many friends here as she had back home in England then. Now she could barely remember a single one of them, and could only shudder at the memory of her last disastrous visit to Marbella.

The car made a sudden turn to the right, driving through a pair of open gates and up the driveway to a private villa. Built on one level, it sprawled hacienda-style right and left of a stone-built archway which took them into a central courtyard.

As soon as the car stopped at an imposing wide framed entrance, Luiz was out of the car and coming around to her side to help her to alight.

'What is this place?' she asked, glancing furtively around the whitewashed vine strewn walls that were now surrounding them. But what really captured her attention was the fleet of other cars all parked up here. Cars meant people, and people meant—

'Luiz!' she protested in dismay when he caught hold of her hand and began pulling her in through the entrance. 'What's going on here?'

'A party,' he said.

Caroline began to wonder if she was losing her sanity. He had just put her through one of the worst evening in her entire life, and now he was casually dragging her off to a party?

'No way,' she refused, tugging to a standstill. 'I don't want to party. And I certainly don't want to do it looking like—this!'

He turned round to look at her, and something very hot suddenly burned in his eyes. 'You look sensational,' he told her huskily.

Sensational? She almost laughed in his face! 'That's the best lie you've told me to date!' she scoffed. 'I've just been swimming. My hair is a mess and I have on no make-up. My skin smells of chlorine and I'm not even wearing a bra!'

He just smiled a sinfully sexy smile and murmured, 'I know. I was there, remember?'

The smile had her floundering—floundering because it was pure *old* Luiz. The one who'd used to smile at her just like that when they'd been passionate lovers and so very at ease together that she would have cut out anyone's tongue if they'd tried to tell her he was using her for a fool!

It played oddly on her defences to remember that. Made her want to relax her guard and smile back at him, be the old Caroline, from when life had been wonderful and she'd been in love and thought she didn't have a single care in the world.

Her hand twitched in his—reacting to secret wishes. His own fingers tightened, as if he thought she was trying to get away and he was making sure that she didn't.

'Luiz…' she pleaded, responding to that glimpse of the man she used to know.

It was like watching warm living tissue turn to stone. 'If you are going to start begging, then don't,' he advised. 'We went way beyond the point where it could be of any use to you to do so, a long time ago.'

When had that point been exactly? she wondered, taking his verbal slap-down with a wince she didn't even bother to try and hide. When they'd been kissing each other into a frenzy in the pool room, perhaps? The twist to her mouth mocked the suggestion, because the man who had all but completely devoured her had recovered too quickly and too well to be vulnerable to anything—including the begging voice of the woman he'd held in his arms at the time.

In his office then, when he had cruelly and efficiently slayed her with words? No room for begging there, she thought grimly. No room for anything but bitterness and anger and pain and…

'Negotiations are over, I take it,' she clipped.

He gave a curt nod. 'All I want from you now is a simple yes or no to my proposition.'

'Your blackmail, you mean,' she countered thinly.

'Okay, blackmail.' He gave an indifferent shrug to her play on words, and took her into a large white hall constructed almost entirely of marble.

A pair of narrow hallways led off to the left and the right of her, linking the separate wings of the villa, she assumed. But it was to one of the rooms directly off this main hallway that Luiz took her.

'Who does this house belong to?' she asked tartly. 'Only I suppose I should know just whose hospitality I will be offending, coming to their party looking like this...'

'Then you don't need to think about it,' Luiz answered pragmatically. 'Since it is me you will be offending.'

In a night of hard shocks, this was just another one to help keep her knocked permanently out of kilter, she supposed, remembering the Luiz of seven years ago telling her smilingly that he lived out of hotels. 'Homes are for families, and I don't have one,' he'd told her casually, but she'd seen the bleakness in his eyes when he'd said it, and known that inside he hadn't been feeling casual at all.

It was a memory that brought with it another question that almost blew her mind apart. 'You're not married now, are you?' she choked out.

His answering burst of laughter took them in through the door and offered no warning whatsoever of what she was about to come face to face with.

Her heart dropped with a sickening thump to the pit of her stomach. The roller coaster ride of emotion she seemed to be on swung her through yet another violently swerving dive. Admittedly, it was a beautiful room, furnished in the very best that was tasteful in Spanish architecture.

But it wasn't the room that held her frozen. Or even the blanket awareness of a couple of dozen people turning in their direction—though their sheer elegance was enough to have her shrinking back to half hide behind Luiz, while sheer vanity sent her fingers up to self-consciously touch her tangle-dried hair.

No, being aware that she must look as if Luiz had just plucked her out of the sea like a mermaid and decided to bring her along here for her novelty value was not what was filling her with a dizzying dismay. It was the sight of a green baize table waiting at the ready, barely three feet away from where she stood, with a solemn-faced croupier standing nearby, counting different coloured gambling chips into neat stacks on a separate counter.

'Where is he?' she whispered, her voice thickened by the actual reality of what Luiz had set up here.

He didn't even try to misunderstand the question. 'In one of the bedrooms,' he replied. 'Taking a rest before the evening begins.'

Begins... The word played back and forth across her frozen senses, her glazed eyes barely seeing the waiting party of people now, even though they were standing there in expectant silence, obviously waiting for Luiz to introduce her.

But Caroline didn't want to be introduced. In fact she felt positively sick with revulsion at the very idea. Because if they were here, and that table was there, then they were all no-good gamblers like her own wretched father. Like the man standing at her side.

And it was decision time, she realised starkly. Now, before this situation got any worse!

Without any further consideration of what she was about to do, she slid herself stealthily round until she was standing directly in front of Luiz. 'All right,' she breathed into his left shoulder.

'All right, what?' he quizzed, aiming a puzzled frown down at her.

'All right. I'll sleep with you,' she whispered. Cold fingers took a fierce grip on his sleeve. 'Now,' she added tautly. 'We'll go and do it right now...'

CHAPTER FOUR

HIS sudden tension suggested that she had just managed to shock him. Caroline didn't care. She wanted out of this room and she wanted her father kept out of it too.

Hard hands suddenly grasped her shoulders, the slender bones almost snapped under the tension she was placing them under. 'Caroline—'

'No!' she interrupted with a choke that was almost a sob. Her mouth was quivering, she couldn't seem to stop it, and her throat was hot and tight. 'Negotiations are over, you told me,' she reminded him. 'You wanted my answer. Well, you've got it. So now get me out of here!'

His chest heaved on the sigh that shot from him; his fingers increased their grip. 'You fool!' he muttered, then, on a complete change of manner, said sardonically to their audience. 'My apologies, but I seem to have inadvertently embarrassed my companion. Please, go on enjoying yourselves while I take her away and attempt to make my peace before I bring her back again.'

The answering rumble of surprise and consternation flicked at her like the stinging tip of a whip. Luiz was smiling back at them through violently gritted teeth. His hands left her shoulders, an arm returning to clamp around them instead. Then he walked her stiff and quivering frame back through the doors, letting them shut behind them.

He was furious with her for causing that scene. Caroline knew that, but had gone way beyond the point where she could do anything about it. The knowledge of what she had just agreed to was clinging like a tight steel band around her aching chest and stopping her from uttering a single word in her own defence.

With a grimness that made her feel like a child being marched off by a stern parent, Luiz took her across the foyer and along the opposite hallway. At the other end was a door that opened into a large bedroom furnished with the same stylish elegance as the other room, only this room had a king-size bed occupying prominent position instead of a card table.

The door closed them in. Caroline stood just in front of it with her head held high and waited to find out what was to come at her next.

Would he order her to take all her clothes off and climb into the bed? Or was he going to offload whatever it was he was keeping severely damped down inside him before he ordered her out of her clothes?

She couldn't see his face because he had his back to her, but she could certainly see his tension. And on one level she was rather satisfied to see that she seemed to have managed to rock the unrockable poise of Luiz Vazquez.

He moved at last, breaking the throbbing silence with a short heavy explosion of air before dipping his hand into one of the pockets of his cream tux. It came out again with her evening bag, which he tossed onto a nearby chair. She'd forgotten he even had it. Next came her black silk bra—which she had forgotten about also. But she was now painfully reminded of their passionate interlude in the pool room as she watched that item land on top of the bag.

He removed his jacket next. It landed on the bed. Broad shoulders, tanned neck, bright white dress shirt made of a fine enough linen for her to see the darkness of his skin showing through. Her heart began to stutter. Her throat went dry. The steel band around her chest tightened its grip a little more. He swung around to look at her appraisingly, making her sharply catch her breath.

She couldn't speak. She was too stressed out to speak. But even if she'd been able to she knew that she wouldn't. She had played her last card. Whatever was left was for Luiz to play.

'You have fifteen minutes to do whatever it takes to make you face my guests without the expression of horror.'

The command utterly threw her. She had expected anger, she had expected seduction, she had even expected a heavy mix of both! But she hadn't expected to feel the slap of his icy contempt.

But her chin tilted even higher, amethyst eyes glinting with a defiance that hid whatever she was feeling inside. 'But I don't want to face your guests in any way,' she stiffly informed him.

'Nevertheless,' he drawled, 'it is what you are going to do.'

'They have nothing to do with what we are here for!' she protested, breaking free from her steel casing when all Luiz did was swing away again, to stride across the room towards a long line of floor-to-ceiling cupboards.

'And it wasn't your friends that filled me with horror,' she added as she followed angrily in his footsteps. 'It was that card table standing there ready and waiting, like a stage prop, for you to play out some hideous act of destruction on my father!'

'You are still assuming that I am going to win, then,' he remarked, opening one of the cupboard doors.

Her footsteps stopped. 'Whether you will or not no longer comes into it!' Despite the anger, her anxiety was beginning to show in the faint tremor of her voice. 'We made a deal where if I sleep with you, you don't play him!

You proposed it, Luiz!' she reminded him. 'And I just agreed!'

In the process of withdrawing a fresh dinner jacket from inside the cupboard, Luiz glanced at her anxious, defiant face, flicked a similar glance at the waiting bed, then smiled the kind of smile that could freeze a fast-flowing river. 'I just upped the ante,' he told her softly. Then calmly shrugged himself into his jacket while Caroline just stood there dumbfounded.

'I d-don't understand...' she stammered. 'W-what do you m-mean?'

Smoothly, he repeated it for her. 'I just upped the ante.' With a deft tug he pulled bright white cuffs with black and gold cufflinks into view. He worded it differently. 'The deal has just changed.'

'But—you can't do that!' she protested.

He looked at her. 'How,' he oh, so tauntingly enquired, 'are you going to stop me?'

'But—I've already agreed to your sordid little deal,' she cried out in complete bewilderment. 'What else can you possibly want from me, Luiz?'

'That's it.' He nodded, as if she'd said something memorably fortuitous. 'Sordid,' he explained. 'I've decided that I don't want sordid.' He moved briskly to check out his bow tie in the sleek gold-framed mirror hanging on the wall above a rosewood tallboy. 'In fact sordid doesn't suit my plans at all, which is why I've decided to up the ante.'

'To what, for goodness' sake?' she asked in pure frustration.

His fingers stilled against the bow tie. Via the mirror he looked at her. Via the mirror his cold, dark inscrutable eyes captured hers. And Caroline found herself holding onto her breath in a way that starved her brain of oxygen during a pause that seemed to go on for ever—before he answered her with the silk-voiced simplistic use of a single word that completely blew her mind.

'Marriage,' he said.

Seconds, minutes—Caroline didn't know how long it was that she just stood there staring at him, as if he was on one planet while she was on another.

Then she gave a shaky laugh. 'You're joking,' she decided.

But his deadly smooth, deadly calm, deadly serious expression told her that this was no joke. He meant it. Marriage. Luiz wanted marriage. To her.

Without a single word, she turned and walked back to the bedroom door. This had gone far enough, she was telling herself grimly. And it had gone on long enough. Now she was—

'We have been here before, Caroline, but I am quite happy to act out the scene again if you need me to do it...' Luiz's voice slid snake-like after her. 'So, walk out of that door and I *will* play your father tonight at poker...'

Her fingers curled around the brass doorhandle, actually gripped and began to turn it before she lost the will. Slowly she turned, weakly she leaned against the door now behind her, defeatedly she stared across the room to where Luiz was now propped up against the rosewood tallboy, with his ankles crossed casually and his hands resting comfortably in his trouser pockets.

Tall, dark, undoubtedly the most attractive man she had ever met in her entire life, he exuded self-assurance from every supremely relaxed pore.

The self-assured kind of man who wanted his pound of flesh, for some utterly obscure reason. 'I suppose you have a good reason for making this proposition?' she prompted shakily.

His lashes flickered, hiding dark brown eyes as they slid over her. 'Yes,' he confirmed.

Caroline's mouth tightened. 'Am I to know what that reason is?' she asked.

'Not until you agree to do it,' he replied. 'And maybe not even then, depending on *how* you agree to it.'

'Then how would you *like* me to agree to it?' she enquired ever so, ever so sweetly, beginning to pulse with anger at the way he was making her pull answers out of him.

A smile touched his mouth, a very wry smile that acknowledged her sarcasm. 'Well, a simple *yes* would do for starters,' he drawled. 'But to hear you say yes because you simply can't imagine the rest of your life without me in it would be absolutely perfect.'

Since the chances of that happening were less than nil, she didn't even bother to remark on the suggestion. 'And what are the chances of the ante going up again before you're finished with me?' she asked instead.

'Finished with you?' Curiously he picked up on the word, then gave a shake of his head. 'In this case, my ever being *finished* with you doesn't apply,' he told her. 'I may sound like a fully emancipated all-American guy,' he said, thickening his accent to suit the remark, 'but remember that I *am* Spanish. And, being Spanish, I marry once and for life. So take that on board while you make your decision,' he advised her. 'I want your *life* Caroline,' he spelled out. 'And, because I have raised the stakes,' he added, 'I will not only *not* play your father tonight, but I will also agree to pay off all his outstanding debts, get your home out of hock and ensure that it remains that way for the rest of your life. At the same time I will take over your watchdog role with your father.' He seemed to decide that covered it nicely. 'Does that sweeten the deal a little for you?'

Sweeten it? It made it positively compelling, she thought with heaviness that took her that little bit closer to defeat—though if she had any choices at all she wished someone would point them out to her. 'If this is for life, then why me?' She frowned, wishing she understood what was really going on. And she knew there just had to be something going on that Luiz wasn't talking about.

'Why not you?' Luiz countered with a shrug. 'You are beautiful, you are well bred, and you would enhance the arm of any man,'

'A trophy, in other words,' she likened bitterly.

'If you like.' He wasn't going to argue with that belittling description. 'But honesty forces me to add that I still fancy the hell out of you or you wouldn't be standing here at all, believe me.'

His dry smile made her flinch. But she received the message well enough. Be glad I do still fancy you, Caroline, or you would now be standing in deep trouble somewhere else entirely.

'Yes. I will marry you,' she said, that briefly and that simply.

To give him credit, Luiz didn't try to draw out his victory. 'Good,' was all he said, then, straightening his lean frame away from the tallboy, turned to slide open the top drawer.

Standing there, watching him, Caroline thought she saw the merest glimpse of a tremor in his hand as he took it out of his pocket to open the drawer. But by the time he turned, with a clean handkerchief in a hand that revealed only super-sure steadiness, she decided that she must have been mistaken.

'You now have ten minutes to make yourself feel better about meeting our guests,' he said, with a subtle alteration in the possessive that didn't pass Caroline by. 'Bathroom through that door.' He indicated. 'Clothes in the cupboards. I have a few phone calls to make.'

With that he began walking towards her, looking the

cool, calm, inscrutable Luiz Vazquez who utterly scorned the idea that anything so weak as a tremor could dare to touch him.

She was blocking the door he obviously wished to go through to make his precious calls, but for the life of her Caroline couldn't give another single inch to him by stepping meekly to one side.

He reached her, stopped. Her heart began to thump. Taller than her, wider than her, darker than her in every way there was, he intimidated her on levels she had not known existed before she knew him.

His eyebrows arched. 'Is there something we missed?' he prompted, softly mocking her stubborn refusal to budge.

She had to swallow through a terrible tension before saying what was on her mind, but she was determined to say it anyway. 'Didn't you hurt me enough seven years ago without continuing this vendetta you seem to have going for my family?'

His hand came up, touched her pale cheek, and the skin beneath began to burn as if branded. 'Seven years ago you would not have needed to ask that question,' he murmured.

'Seven years ago I thought you loved me,' she replied huskily. 'But it wasn't love, was it, Luiz? I was merely there, and easy, which provided you with a bit of light amusement in between all the really serious stuff.'

He smiled an odd smile. 'Is that what you think?'

'It's what I know,' she insisted—even now, seven years on, still able to feel the bitterness of learning that eating away at her.

His dark head came down, making her stiffen and tingle when he brought his lips into contact with her ear. 'Then how can you bear to have me touch you?' he whispered in soft, moist, sensual derision—and dropped his fingers from her cheek to place them over her breast where the thin fabric of her dress did nothing to disguise her instant response to him.

With a jerk she stepped sideways and right out of his reach, hating herself and despising him so much that she could barely cope with what was now tumbling about inside her.

Luiz said nothing, but then he really didn't need to—which was the real humiliation as he simply opened the door she was no longer guarding and stepped through it.

Left alone, it was all she could do just to sink weakly into the nearest chair. Instantly she felt something beneath her, and reached down and plucked out both her bag and her bra. The flimsy piece of black silk dangled like a taunt from her trembling fingers, reminding her why it wasn't on her body.

It was still slightly damp. On another thought she got up and walked over to the bed, where Luiz had dropped his discarded jacket. The moment she picked it up the clean scent of him began to completely surround her. Her eyes were still glazed but her other senses were working just fine, she noted grimly. For touching this jacket was like touching Luiz. Smelling him, feeling him, wanting him—wanting him...

The jacket, like her bra, was damp, which was obviously why Luiz had changed it for another one. Damp around the pocket, where he'd stuffed her bra, damp around the shoulders from when he'd placed it around hers.

A sigh whispered from her that was so bleak and hopeless she was glad there was no one around to hear it. Seven weeks loving him, she thought sadly. Seven years hating him. And probably only seven seconds back in his presence and she had been fighting a losing battle against the way he could make her feel.

It was awful, like coming face to face with her own

darkest secret. For hate was merely the other side of love. Weren't the romantics always saying that?

Which left her with what to comfort herself? she wondered as she dropped all three items on the bed and turned her back on them. She didn't know—didn't think she wanted to know.

The clothes he had told her she would find in the cupboards happened to be her own clothes, which brought home even harder the amount of calculation he had put into all of this. He had been very sure of himself, very positive that she would end up here with him, one way or another.

In fact everything she had brought to Marbella with her was now residing in this room. Except for her father, she added—then instantly began to worry about him, maybe wandering about this villa like a loose cannon searching for some explosive excitement.

The prospect had her hurrying to change. She spent less than five minutes in the well-equipped bathroom, showering away the effects of her swim and then hurriedly blowdrying her hair before she applied a quick, light covering of make-up and went to decide what she was going to wear.

Luiz arrived back as she was slipping her feet into high patent leather shoes. Her chin-length bob was soft and shiny, her make-up underplayed, and her dress was made of dark purple silk crêpe, with a neckline that scooped down to caress the soft swell of her breasts and skimmed rather than clung to the rest of her curves.

Dramatically simplistic it its design, still the dress did things for her that made his eyes glint beneath the heavy shading of those long lashes he so liked to hide behind.

'I'm impressed,' he said. 'I didn't think you could do it in the time allocated.'

Caroline just sent him a coldly dismissive look. 'Is my father awake yet?'

'It's almost midnight, Caroline,' Luiz drawled back lazily. 'The time people usually go to bed, not think about getting up.'

'People don't usually throw parties this late, either,' she pointed out.

He smiled at the curt censure. 'I'm an owl.'

'So is he,' she countered. 'Where is he?'

'In the kitchen playing blackjack with the chef,' he replied laconically—then, at her look of slack-jawed horror, he grew angry. 'For goodness' sake!' he bit out. 'It was a joke!'

Some joke, she thought painfully.

Luiz strode forward; a hard hand grabbed one of hers. 'He's comfortably ensconced in the main salon enjoying the company of my guests!' he told her impatiently. 'Will you lighten up?'

Lighten up? she repeated furiously. She was tired, she was stressed, she had just gone through some of the worst few hours in her entire life—and he was now demanding that she *lighten up?*

'If I had a punch worth throwing I would probably hit you,' she whispered.

With a heavy sigh, Luiz pulled her towards him, and it showed how bad she was feeling that she let him hold her against his chest. 'He's fine,' he assured her huskily. 'And he will stay fine now that I'm looking after him—I thought you understood that.'

'He's an addict, Luiz,' she stated with heart slaying honesty. 'They don't get cured overnight.'

'I know,' he said quietly.

'Does *he* know?' she then asked sharply. 'About this deal you and I have just made?'

'He knows you are here with me, but that's about all.'

Which made just one more problem she still had yet to confront, she thought heavily, and moved right out of Luiz's arms. His eyes narrowed on her weary profile, but he didn't try to detain her.

Instead he moved back to the door, then stood waiting for her to join him. Caroline did so without uttering another word. As they walked side by side back towards the main salon she thought she could actually feel the vibration of her own body it was so beset by nerve-tingling tension.

'Do I get to know who any of these people are before I have to meet them?' she asked without much hope of an answer, since he was very economical with those.

'Nervous?' Luiz questioned as they crossed the foyer.

'Yes,' she confessed.

'Then don't be.' He sounded eminently confident of that. 'You are about to meet my family,' he told her. 'Not a firing squad.'

His *family*? 'But you told me once that you don't have any family!' She stared at him in disbelief.

He just smiled another odd smile. 'I don't,' he said, but the sudden cold glitter that struck his eyes sent a chill chasing down her spine.

'Enigmatic as ever, I note,' she drawled.

He responded with a different smile. 'My secret weapon,' he admitted.

But not his only one, she thought as she felt his hand make contact with the small of her back as the other hand reached out for the door. His touch stung through her like an electric power source, making her spine arch fiercely.

Her reaction made him pause, his features hardening. 'Just remember who you are and *what* you are to me when we walk in there,' he warned very grimly. 'It is very important to me that you give a good impression of a blissful bride, not a resentful one.'

Refusing to look at him, Caroline said nothing. But her chin dutifully lifted and her expression became smooth as he pushed open the door to the main salon.

The first thing her eyes went to was the green baize table, which she was relieved to see had been deftly covered with a white linen tablecloth on which several bottles of champagne now lay, chilling on a bed of ice. And the croupier, who had been stacking coloured chips earlier, now stood polishing fluted champagne glasses with the innocence of a waiter.

The next thing she allowed her eyes to take in was the room full of people. What she had seen only as a couple of dozen blurred faces the first time around, now became two dozen separate individuals who were, almost without exception, Spanish.

'Highborn' and 'haughty' were the mocking words that came to mind to describe the way they were looking back at her. Which then made her think that if these people were related to Luiz, then he had to come from some very rare stock. Some young, some old, some distinctly curious, some noticeably cautious, she noted. But what struck her the fiercest were the waves of antipathy she could feel bouncing off them, even though she could sense they were trying hard to hide it.

They don't like Luiz, she realised on a blinding flash of insight. They might be here in his home, enjoying his champagne and his hospitality, but they resent it for some baffling reason.

Which served to further confuse a situation that was already muddled enough.

Then, at last, she noticed her father, standing slightly apart from the others and seemingly not at all pleased, by the look on his face. He was frowning into the whisky glass he held in his hand instead of bothering to glance their way, as everyone else had done the moment the doors had opened.

She knew what he was thinking. He was thinking— When the hell, with all these people around, am I going to get my game of poker? Because that was the way his mind worked when he was in the grip of his personal madness.

Well, he is about to receive a rather nasty surprise! she predicted with no sympathy for him whatsoever. He had let her down tonight, let her down so badly that it was going to be hard for her to forgive him this time.

This time—she repeated. How many 'this times' had there been over the last ten years?

And how many more were there going to be? Plenty, she predicted, despite Luiz's grand promise.

'Really, Luiz.' A rather large-boned lady, wearing a very regal magenta silk gown, decided to break the silence with haughty censure. 'I am too old to be indulging in late-night parties. Do you see the time? Do you realise how unforgivably rude you have been, summoning us all here then leaving us to kick our heels while we await your pleasure?'

'My apologies, Aunt Beatriz,' Luiz murmured, seeming not to notice the contempt in the older woman's tone. 'But I was so sure you wouldn't want to miss this particular party once you knew the reason for it.'

'Reason—what reason?' Still cross, but curious, the aunt fixed him with a stern glare.

'A celebration,' Luiz replied—deliberately, Caroline was sure, titillating everyone's senses with carefully chosen words. 'Of my incredible good fortune...'

The moment he said it Caroline's chest felt tight again, responding to what she knew was about to come. Luiz's hand slid from her back to her waistline, but whether it was offering warning or support she wasn't certain. And her father's head came up, eyes that were more grey than amethyst fixing sharply on his daughter.

'In the full tradition of the Vazquez family,' Luiz was saying smoothly beside her, 'I have brought you all here to introduce you to Miss Caroline Newbury. The lady who has just promised to be my bride—and my future Condesa...'

After that kind of announcement it was difficult to say who was more utterly dumbfounded. His family or Caroline herself. Caroline was certainly swinging dizzily off balance yet again—because to be Luiz's future Condesa meant that Luiz had to be the Conde!

Her heart gave a thudding kick, sending shock waves rampaging throughout her whole system. As she watched, having no ability left to do much else, she saw two dozen faces drop. It was terrible. The whole situation was utterly terrible. Not so much for her but for Luiz. Did none of these people have a single nice thing to say to him? Could they not at least pretend delight at his news? They didn't know that Luiz wasn't head over heels in love with his newly betrothed!

And further back, standing apart from the others, was her father, his expression completely frozen. He had caught on quickly, Caroline realised. He might be self-obsessed most of the time, but he wasn't stupid. He knew that if Luiz was announcing his intention to marry his daughter, then she had sold herself to him for the price of her father's debts.

'No.' She saw his mouth form the denial, and tears began to clog her throat.

Then one voice—just one voice in a wilderness of silence—sighed and said, 'Congratulations.' A woman about her father's age stepped forward. 'And to think we all thought when you had us gather here tonight that you were about to surrender your title and go back to America!'

Hoped, Caroline grimly corrected as she felt the atmosphere in the room change from hidden hostility to forced elation in one violent swing. After that they were buried beneath a sea of congratulations, and she found herself struggling to keep up with the names and the embraces being thrust her way. Champagne corks began to pop. The waiter-cum-croupier began handing out glasses for everyone to share a toast.

While still standing apart from it all was her father, Caroline noticed anxiously. He was staring at her as if a veil had been ripped from his eyes and he was seeing clearly for the first time in years. It frightened her, that look, as did the way his face seemed to be getting greyer with each passing second that went by.

'Luiz—my father,' she murmured, an inner sense warning her that something dire was about to happen. But even as she caught Luiz's attention, she saw, to her horror, her father's fingers let go of the whisky glass so it dropped with a thud to the carpet. 'No, Daddy. No!' she cried out as his face began to distort and his hand went up to clutch at his chest just before he began to crumple.

CHAPTER FIVE

THE rest became a blur, a cold, dark, muddy blur, where Luiz leapt from her side to catch hold of her father just before he hit the ground. The croupier-cum-waiter leapt also, and between the two of them they managed to get his limp body onto one of the sofas, while Caroline just stood there, lost in the fog of one terrifying shock too many.

I did this, she was thinking over and over. I've just killed my own father. She couldn't move a single muscle, while someone else—a perfect stranger to her, though she must have met him just now amongst the confusing melee—strode briskly over to the sofa and knelt down to examine her father.

The way Luiz immediately deferred to him was telling her something she was incapable of understanding just then. But she watched as if from behind a pane of glass as the man's long fingers checked the pulse in her father's neck before he began quickly untying his bow tie then releasing the top few buttons to his dress shirt.

'Vito—my bag, from my car, if you please,' he commanded.

The man who'd jumped to her father's aid along with Luiz now quickly left the room, and an arm came carefully around Caroline's trembling shoulders.

It was the lady in magenta. 'Be calm,' she murmured gruffly. 'My husband is a doctor. He will know what to do.'

'H-he suffers f-from angina.' The information literally shivered from Caroline's paralysed throat. 'He sh-should

73

have pills to take in h-his pocket. Daddy!' she cried out, as at last she broke free of her paralysis and went to go to him.

But Luiz's aunt held her back. 'Let Fidel do his job, child,' she advised. Then, with a calmness that belied everything happening around her, she relayed the information Caroline had just given her to her husband, the doctor.

Luiz's head shot round, his dark eyes lashing over Caroline as if she had just revealed some devilish secret aimed specifically to wound him. She didn't understand. Not the accusing look, or the blistering anger that came along with it. And he was as white as a sheet—as white as her father was frighteningly grey!

The slide of pills found, the doctor quickly read the prescription printed across them. By then his bag had arrived at his side and he was demanding Luiz's attention, instructing him to take off her father's jacket and roll up his shirtsleeve so he could place a blood pressure pad around his arm. While Luiz was doing that, the doctor was listening to her father's heart.

It was all very efficient, very routine to him, probably. But to Caroline it was the worst—very worst thing she had ever experienced in her entire life. She'd done this, she was thinking guiltily. She had done this to him by not insisting on breaking Luiz's deal to him in private and in her own less brutal way.

But she hadn't cared. Not until she had seen his face just now. She had been angry with him, and bitter, and had actually wanted to shock him into seeing what he had finally brought her to!

But what she had brought him to by far outweighed what he'd done to her.

'He is beginning to come round,' Luiz's aunt murmured.

The doctor was talking quietly to him and Luiz was still squatting beside them, his dark face honed into the hardest mask Caroline had ever seen it wear. And everyone else stood about, looking and feeling helpless, while right there in the middle of a beautiful cream carpet her father's glass still lay on its side in a pool of golden liquid.

She saw one of her father's hands move, going up to cover his eyes. He looked old and frail and pathetically vulnerable lying there, and as her heart cracked wide open she shook herself free from the comforting arm and went to him.

'Daddy...' she sobbed. She felt Luiz glance at her, then grimly straighten up to make room for her to take his place beside his uncle. Her hand went out, the fingers ice-cold and trembling as they closed around her father's then gently pulled his hand away from his eyes. 'I'm so sorry,' she whispered thickly.

'It was a shock, that's all,' he answered weakly. 'Didn't expect it. Forgot to take my pill today. My fault. I'll be all right again in a few minutes.'

The doctor was waiting with blood-pressure pad at the ready once the pill had been given a chance to take effect. Caroline flicked him an anxiously questioning look and he answered it with a small nod. Relief flooded the tears into her eyes.

Her father saw them and his grey face looked weary. 'Don't weep for me, Caroline,' he sighed. 'I have enough to contend with right now, without adding your tears.'

'But it's all my fault,' she choked. 'I should have warned you about Luiz and me. It was—'

'Supposed to be a pleasant surprise for all of you,' Luiz grimly put in, still aware of their audience, and protecting his damned deal from the risk of exposure even in the face of all of this, Caroline realised bitterly.

Her father seemed to understand and accept that. His tired eyes lifted to Luiz. 'We need to talk,' he murmured grimly.

'Not tonight, though,' the doctor decreed. 'For tonight you will be staying as my personal guest in my private hospital.'

And even as he spoke the sound of a siren whined its way into the room, curdling Caroline's blood and making her cling tightly to her father's hand. But what really worried her was that her father didn't attempt to put in a protest.

His eyes fluttered open. 'Don't look so stricken.' He smiled at her wearily. 'I plan to be a thorn in your side for a long time yet.'

'Promise?' she insisted with the kind of painful seriousness that had those who witnessed it lowering their eyes.

'I promise,' he ruefully complied. Then to Luiz, who was standing behind Caroline, 'Not quite the response you were looking for, I think,' he drawled.

'No,' Luiz quietly agreed.

'Does she know yet?'

'Know what?' Caroline put in sharply.

But on a wince her father closed his eyes again, and all conversation came to a standstill as the doctor began pumping up the blood pressure pad wrapped around his arm.

Two medics entered the room then, and Luiz was gently drawing Caroline to her feet, to make way for them so they could do what they had to do unencumbered. But the moment the medics began to move her father onto their mobile stretcher she was back at his side. The rest of the people in the room had slithered off into the ether. She neither saw them nor wanted to see them.

The drive to the hospital was undertaken with the minimum of fuss. Caroline travelled with her father in the ambulance while Luiz followed behind in his car. After that everything became a worried blur again as they waited while her father was put through several examinations before Luiz's uncle Fidel eventually came to pass on the reassuring news that it had not been a heart attack as such. 'But his blood pressure has remained a little high,' he added. 'So I am going to keep him in here overnight, just to keep an eye on him.'

With a sinking sense of profound relief, Caroline leaned weakly against the wall behind her. But when Luiz attempted to touch her she shrugged him off abruptly. 'I'm all right,' she said.

'You don't damn well look it,' he argued gruffly.

Ignoring him, she looked at his uncle. 'Can I see him now?' she asked.

'For a few moments only,' she was told. 'He is sedated, so he will not know you are here.'

They did stay for only a few moments, for as the doctor had said he was asleep, but his colour was much better. Caroline stood by his bed gently stroking his hand for a few minutes while Luiz looked on in silence from his position at the bottom of the bed. Then, with the helplessness that came from knowing that she could do nothing more by remaining there, she allowed Luiz to take her away.

They didn't speak as they walked through the hospital, but then they had barely exchanged a single word since the whole horror had begun in Luiz's drawing room. They reached the exit doors to find Luiz's uncle was waiting for them.

He glanced gravely from one face to the other—seeing too much maybe; Caroline wasn't sure. 'He is going to be fine,' he assured her gently. 'It really was only a small scare.'

'Yes, I know...' Nodding, Caroline fought yet another battle with tears, then impulsively stepped up to embrace Luiz's uncle. 'Thank you for being there,' she whispered simply.

'It was my pleasure,' he replied, but his attention was

fixed on her own drained pallor. 'Take her home,' he said to Luiz. 'Make her go to bed, and don't allow her to come back here until lunchtime at the earliest.'

They left almost immediately after that. The black BMW was waiting in the car park. Luiz had driven himself to the hospital, Caroline discovered when, after seeing her into the front passenger seat, he climbed in behind the wheel.

His expression was closed, and he still didn't speak as he set the car in motion. Outside it was dark and very quiet now, the hour one of those ungodly ones where even the owls Luiz likened himself to had retired.

'I want to go back to the hotel,' she said—and received no answer. Turning her head to look at him, she saw only that closed cast of a profile. 'Luiz...' she prompted.

He changed gear and turned the steering wheel to take them off the main road which would have taken them back into Puerto Banus. He had the long, brown, skilful fingers of an accomplished magician, she found herself thinking stupidly. And she knew she was only letting her mind notice his hands because she didn't want to get into another heated row with him.

Yet she couldn't let the subject go. 'I don't want to face all those people again,' she told him.

He decided to answer that one. 'They've gone home.' His voice was quiet, flat, utterly devoid of any inflexion when he added, 'The party, I think you would agree, is well and truly over.'

'Did it ever get started?' she shot at him tartly. If 'party' was the right word to cover whatever it was Luiz had been hoping to set up tonight. In truth, the man's motives baffled her. His family baffled her. One moment they'd appeared hostile and resentful, the next too ecstatic to be real.

'They don't like you,' she said continuing her thought pattern out loud.

'They haven't had time yet to make up their mind,' he answered levelly.

Caroline frowned. 'What does that mean?'

'It means I've only been an entity in their lives for a few months.' In profile she caught the slight hint of a grimace. 'Since my father died, in fact,' he tagged on, 'and it was revealed that he had left his estates, his money and his title to the bastard son they'd all preferred to pretend never existed.'

Sitting there beside him, Caroline took her time absorbing this information, because it helped explain so many other things about Luiz that had been a mystery to her until then.

'Did you know about him?' she questioned softly.

'Yes,' he said.

'Always?'

'More or less,' he replied. Economical and to the point.

'But he never acknowledged you until recently,' she therefore concluded.

Luiz turned the car in through the gates of the villa and drove them beneath the arch into the courtyard. As the engine went silent neither tried to get out of the car. Caroline because she sensed there was more information coming, and Luiz because he was, she suspected, deciding how much he wanted to tell her.

'He tried, once,' he admitted. 'Seven years ago, to be exact. But it—didn't come to anything.'

Seven years ago. Seven. Caroline's lungs suddenly ceased to work. 'Why?' she whispered.

Luiz turned to look at her, his closely guarded eyes flickering over her pale, tired, now wary face, and it was like being bathed in a shower of static. For, whatever he was thinking while he looked at her like that, she knew without a single doubt that his thoughts belonged seven years in his past and most definitely included her.

Then he flicked his eyes away. 'He wasn't what I wanted,' he declared, and opened his door and climbed out of the car, leaving Caroline to sit there, making what she liked of that potentially earth-shattering statement.

Was he was talking about her? Was he talking about them? Was he talking about seven years ago, when he must have been here in Marbella to meet his father and had instead got himself involved with an English girl and her gambling father?

Her door came open. Luiz bent down to take hold of her arm to help urge her out. She arrived beside him in a fresh state of high tension, trembling, afraid to dare let herself draw the most logical conclusions from her own shock questions.

But Luiz couldn't have meant that *she* had been what he had wanted seven years ago, she decided, or he would not have fleeced her father dry at the gambling tables the way he had done.

'Come on,' he murmured gruffly. 'You've taken enough for one night.'

Yes, he was right; she had taken enough, she agreed as a throbbing took up residence behind her eyes. She didn't want to think any more, didn't want to do anything but crawl into the nearest bed and fall asleep.

The house was in darkness. Luiz touched a couple of wall switches as they entered and bathed the hallways in subdued light, then led the way to the bedroom.

Once inside, she didn't seem to have energy left to even undress herself. Luiz watched as she sank wearily down onto the edge of the bed and covered her aching eyes. After a few moments he moved across the room to begin opening cupboards, then she heard his footsteps crossing the cool marble floor towards her and something silky landed on her lap.

Drawing her hand away from her eyes, she saw her own

smoke-grey silk nightdress. With a cool disregard for her utter bone-weariness, he pulled her to her feet and aimed her towards the bathroom. 'Wash, change,' he instructed.

She went on automatic pilot, and came back a few minutes later to find that Luiz was no longer there and that the bedcovers had been turned back ready for her to crawl between. She did so without hesitation. She was just sinking into a blissful oblivion when the door opened and he came back in.

The distinctive clink of ice against glass brought her gritty eyes open in time to watch him place a jug of iced water on the bedside table, along with a couple of glasses, then he strode off to shut himself away behind the bathroom door without uttering a single word.

Caroline lay there, not sure if she should be jumping up and making a run for it while she had the chance, or whether she should just give in to everything and let him do whatever it was he had planned to come next.

She didn't run, was too tired to run. And his *next,* was to reappear wearing nothing but a short black robe that exposed more of his tanned skin than it covered. He brought the clean scent of soap into the room with him—and a heightening of tension because he looked so damned sexually sure of himself, the way he obviously thought he could climb into this bed with her—and naked, by the looks of things!

'I won't sleep with you,' she informed him flatly.

He was hanging his clothes away in the cupboard when she spoke, but he paused, glanced at her. 'Sleep as in *sleep?*' he asked. 'Or sleep as in make love?'

'Both,' she replied. 'And I don't know how you've got the arrogance to think that I would.'

He didn't answer that one straight away. Instead he went back to what he had been doing while Caroline followed his every movement with a heart that was trying hard not to beat any faster.

It didn't succeed very well—especially when he turned towards the bed and began to approach. And his face was wearing that hard, implacable look she didn't like very much. Bending down, he braced himself with one hand on the pillow beside her head and one right by her curled-up knees. He looked very dark, very dangerous—and very, very serious.

'Let's just get a couple of things straight, Caroline,' he suggested quietly and chillingly. 'As far as I am concerned our deal still stands. If you decide not to go through with it, then you know the consequences. They haven't changed because your father was taken ill,' he pointed out. 'But,' he then added, 'if you decide to keep your side of our bargain, then I will expect you to convince your father, and everyone else for that matter, that I am what you want more than anything else in your life. Understand?'

Yes, she thought dully, she understood. Her choices here were still non-existent. 'If anything happens to him,' she said thickly, 'you know I'll never forgive you, don't you?'

He allowed himself a small grimace at that. 'I think I had already worked that one out for myself,' he replied dryly.

'And if you try to touch me now, tonight, I shall probably be sick.'

This time it wasn't a grimace but a weary sigh, and his dark head came closer—close enough for her to feel the warmth of his breath caress her face. 'If I touched you now, Caroline, you would probably burst into tears—then cling to me as though your life depended on it,' he taunted softly.

And to prove his point he brushed his mouth across her mouth. Sure enough, even as he straightened away, the tears were flooding into her eyes.

And she didn't feel sick. She felt—vulnerable. Too vulnerable to say another word as Luiz reached out to flick a switch that plunged the room into darkness. A few seconds later there was a rustling of fabric before she felt the other side of the bed depress.

He didn't attempt to reach for her, didn't try to cross the invisible barrier that ran down the centre of the large bed. She fell asleep still struggling with a mix of emotions ranging from the bitterly resentful to the wretchedly disgusted with herself—because he was right, and she did want to cling to him.

She awoke during what was left of the night, though she wasn't sure what it was that had woken her. But in those few drifting moments before she remembered just where she was, she was only aware that she was lying on her stomach, sprawled diagonally across the bed, feeling so sublimely at peace with herself that it came as a shock to realise that not only was it Luiz's bed she was lying in, but that her cheek was pressed up against his satin-smooth shoulder and her arm was lying across his hair-roughened chest.

And, worse, he was awake. She knew he was because he was lying there on his back, letting his fingers stroke feather-light caresses along her resting arm. It wasn't a sexual gesture; she knew that instinctively. More an absent stroking, as if he was lying there maybe staring into the darkness, lost deep in his own train of thought.

It was nice.

So nice in fact that she didn't really want to end it. Though she didn't know if she could simply go on lying here pretending to be asleep when she wasn't, because already she could feel her pulse-rate picking up, feel the even tempo of her breathing alter.

It was a long time since she'd last felt the warm strength of a man lying beside her. Seven long lonely years, in fact.

And even then it had been *this* man. This same dark, sensually attractive man, with the same clean, slightly musky scent that was so intoxicatingly familiar.

It seemed ironic now, to find herself in this situation when it was Luiz who had spoiled her from wanting to go to bed with another man.

He released a small sigh. Caroline wished that she could do the same, only she knew it would give the game away. Then her defences would have to go back up, the tension would return, the need to keep on fighting him.

The sigh escaped anyway, so she tried to use it as an excuse to slide away, as if in her sleep. Luiz moved at the same time, his fingers tangling with her fingers at the same moment that he rolled onto his side and towards her. She wasn't quick enough to close her eyes, and it was like looking into a mirror and seeing her own sombre mood reflected back at her. Only his eyes were dark—as dark as the night still surrounding them.

He wanted her, she could see the need written there. And the mirror was in knowing that she wanted him. Too late to pretend. Too late to run and hide. He knew just as she knew. It was that simple, that final.

With the use of their tangled fingers he drew her up against him, and even as she felt the aroused heat of his body pushing gently against her his mouth was hungrily capturing hers.

And—oh, but it felt good, like finding something she had been mourning the loss of for too, too long. And perhaps because she didn't fight him, didn't even try to protest, he savoured the kiss, almost as if he was feeling the same way about it as she.

Or maybe it had more to do with the lateness of the hour, their slumberous state, the relaxed warmth with which they had come together, or even that all-encompassing darkness itself.

Whatever, this kiss was like no other kiss they had ever shared. It was slow and it was deep and it was unbelievably tender. And it went on and on and on, until she felt as if she were floating, lost to a beauty so profound that she had to reach up with her free hand and cup his cheek—just to check that he wasn't a mere figment of her dreamy imagination.

Her fingers found lean, taut flesh that rasped lightly with a five o'clock shadow. She touched his cheekbone, his nose, the corner of his mouth where it covered her own mouth, heard his low groan as if her exploration moved him.

Gently rolling her onto her back, he came with her, untangled his fingers from hers and began to touch her face in the self-same way. But the kiss began to alter, subtly at first, then with a deepening of sensuality that quickened the senses.

Linking her hands around his nape, she held him, and his touch begin to drift on a gentle exploration of her throat, her shoulders, and finally the satin-smooth slopes of her waiting breasts. As he brushed a caress across tightly budding peaks she gasped her response into his mouth. One of his hands began to dip low over her ribcage, and as she arched in response to his so-light caress he reached up, caught hold of one of her own hands and fed it onto his body.

It was a command for her to match his movements. She remembered it from the last time they'd come together like this. Luiz had been her tutor in the art of arousing a lover. What he made her feel, he wanted to feel; what he did to her to make her go wild with pleasure, he expected her to do to him.

But that had been seven years ago, and seven years of abstinence had made her unsure of herself. Her fingers fluttered uncertainly against his hair-roughened breastbone,

found one small tight male nipple and began a tentativ
rolling of it between thumb and finger which had hir
groaning thickly. He wrenched his mouth from hers so h
could string a line of heated kisses across her cheek an
down her throat until he found and fixed on one of he
own tightly drawn peaks.

She cried out. It was such a wildly exhilarating sensa
tion. He muttered something she didn't catch, ran his han
down her body, lifting eager nerve-ends to the surface o
her skin as he did so, then caught hold of the hem of he
nightdress and deftly slipped it up and over her head.

With the silk gone, his fingers began tracing the sensi
tive flesh along her inner thigh. Her mouth fixed on hi
shoulder; his returned to her breast. She could feel the hea
of him, the burning, burgeoning power of him, pulsatin
against her hipbone.

His hand was beginning to trail ever further upwards
and she knew that if he touched her where he intended t
go next then he would expect her to touch him the sam
way. But—

'Luiz…' she breathed, needing something—reassuranc
maybe, or even a reprieve. She wasn't really sure.

'Shh,' he commanded, deep, dark, tense with arousal.

Did he think she was about to call a halt to it all? sh
wondered. But that was as far as it got—a question form
ing inside her head—before he literally sent her topplin
over the edge as, with needle-point accuracy, he locate
the very life-force of her.

It threw her into a paroxysm of gasps and whimpers
No warning, no mercy. She hovered precariously on th
very edge of orgasm, and as if he knew it Luiz uttered
soft curse, caught her mouth again with a hard, hot, urgen
kiss that mimicked what he was doing to her. Then he wa
covering her body with his own and positioning himsel
so he could enter her with a sure, sleek thrust.

Delicate tissue unused to this kind of intrusion tensed in a moment's protest at his potent demand. Then she sighed softly, slowly relaxed the tension out of her thighs so that she could draw him in deeper. He responded with a husky groan. After that it became a powerful example of intimacy at its most intense level. Mouth close to mouth, breast to breast, hip to taut hip, they began to move as a single entity. Her hands clutched at his silk taut back while his held her possessively beneath him. Her breath shivered from her parted lips to mingle sensually with his. And with her eyes captured by the burn in his everything else was temporarily forgotten. Past betrayals, present mistrusts—nothing else seemed to matter but what they were feeling.

And feel it they did—together—together so perfectly that when her breathing grew shorter and her body more anxious he knew the exact moment she was about to leap, and drove them over the edge with a fierceness that was completely soul-shattering.

Afterwards, when it was eventually over and Luiz lay heavy on top of her with his face buried in her throat, there was even something perfectly shared in the way neither seemed able to move or speak. Nevertheless, Caroline was glad of the darkness to hide away in when Luiz did eventually find the strength to move. Rolling onto his side, he took her with him, holding her with arms that gave her no room to escape.

'You're mine now,' he said, and that was all.

Caroline didn't even bother to answer. For it didn't take genius for her to work out that she had always been his, even during seven years of never setting eyes on him.

CHAPTER SIX

THE next time she woke it was to find a voile-defused daylight eddying around her. She was alone, she realised, lying sprawled naked on her stomach once again, amongst a sea of tumbled white linen, with her arm thrown out in a way that told her exactly what it had been thrown across until that warm male body had slid stealthily out from beneath it.

Her heart performed a dramatic flip, the memory of the previous twenty-four hours enough to hold her still with her eyes closed tight while she tried to come to terms with knowing just how easy she had been for him.

It was scary. Because even as she coped with the inevitable clutches of shame that knowledge brought with it she was also aware of a gentle pulsing deep inside that was warm and soft and infinitely sensual as delicate muscles searched for the silken force which had given them so much.

'Luiz...' she breathed, then wished she hadn't, because even whispering his name was a sensual experience.

I should hate him, she told herself. I *want* to hate him for doing this to me again. No wonder it all felt so very scary.

A light tap sounded on the bedroom door then, jolting her into a sitting position in the middle of the bed. She had just managed to scramble a white sheet around her nakedness when the door came open and a young woman appeared carrying a breakfast tray.

She was smiling shyly. *'Buenos días, señorita,'* she murmured politely. 'Don Luiz instructed me to waken you in time to meet him at the hospital at noon.'

Noon. Hospital—her father! Oh, dear God, how could she have forgotten him as thoroughly as she had? She was about to leap from the bed in panic when the little maid added, '*El señor* also say to tell you that your *papá* is well, and will be discharged later on today.'

And as Caroline sat, needing long seconds to take this reassuring information in, the girl walked forward and put the tray down on a small table, then turned to enquire if there was anything else she wanted.

'Er, no—thank you,' she answered politely. But as the young maid walked back to the door, a sudden thought hit her. 'Did *el sẽnor* leave the address of the hospital?' she asked. 'Only I forgot to make a note of it in the panic last night.'

'He has placed Señor Martinez at your disposal,' the maid explained. 'He will know where he is to drive you.'

With that she was gone, leaving Caroline to wonder just who Señor Martinez was. The maid seemed to think that Caroline already knew.

She soon found out an hour later, when, dressed casually in soft doe-coloured trousers and a pale pink V-necked top, she stepped into the villa courtyard and found the croupier-cum-waiter and now chauffeur standing waiting for her by the black BMW.

'Good morning, Miss Newbury,' he greeted politely. Deep-voiced, smooth-toned, he had the same pleasant American drawl as Luiz.

Which made him—what, specifically? she wondered as she watched him move to open the rear door of the car for her. Luiz's personal bodyguard? His jack-of-all-trades assistant? His friend?

The very suggestion of Luiz possessing a genuine, slap-on-the-back kind of friend made her smile as she sank into squashy soft leather. He wasn't the type. Luiz was a man who stood alone and softened his guard for no one. Even when he made love he did so with a silent intensity that protected the inner man.

She shivered, not liking it. Not liking what he had been able to expose in her while keeping himself hidden. So, he enjoyed making love with her, she acknowledged with a shrug. She would have to be a fool to have missed the power behind the passion with which he had taken her. But he'd done it in silence. And even his climax had been a disturbingly silent thing that had kept whatever he was experiencing locked deep inside him.

So Señor Martinez couldn't be Luiz's friend, she concluded, because to a man like Luiz a friend would be seen as a weakness.

And, likewise, Señor Martinez didn't look like anyone's idea of a friend, she mused as she watched him settle his bulky size behind the wheel of the car. He had the cold face and tough body of a ruthless terminator—with a hint of the savage thrown in to add extra sinister impact.

All of which she was given the chance to consider only as long as it took him to set the car engine running then send up the partitioning piece of glass.

Shut out and shut in, she thought, and grimaced. Maybe they were brothers after all.

Her father's room was on the second floor. Her feet trod spotless laminated wood flooring and she became aware of an increase of tension as the moment came closer when she was going to have to face her father with the truth— it was no use trying to pretend.

He knew too much—knew her, knew Luiz, and he knew himself. It was being that aware of all involved parties that had put him in here in the first place. What she didn't want was to risk the same thing happening again once he'd heard the full story.

So, nervously she approached the room he had been allotted. The door was standing open; beyond it everything looked clean and neat. She saw Luiz first, standing gazing out of the window. With the sunlight streaming in around him he looked bigger and leaner and more intimidating than usual.

A force to be reckoned with, she likened with a small shudder. And had no concept whatsoever of how prophetic that thought was as she took a moment to brace herself, then stepped into the room proper.

He heard her and spun round, then went very still, watching her face as she glanced expectantly at the bed and began to frown when she found it empty. The room had its own bathroom. She looked next in its direction, saw the room inside was also empty, then finally—reluctantly—flicked her eyes towards Luiz.

'Where is he?' she asked, sounding afraid even to herself.

'It's okay,' he said. 'He hasn't had a relapse.'

Relief made her mouth tremble. 'Then where is he?' she repeated.

There was a lot to be said for having the sunlight behind him, she found herself thinking as she waited for an answer. At least with his face thrown into contrasting shadow she couldn't tell what kind of expression he was wearing, didn't have to guess what he was thinking as he stood there looking at her for the first time since they'd shared his bed.

'Luiz?' she prompted when she realised he still hadn't answered her question.

'He isn't here,' he told her quietly.

Isn't here? Isn't where? Her frown grew more puzzled. 'You mean—he's gone for more tests or something?'

The dark head shook and he took a couple of steps towards her. The moment he did it Caroline was having to

fight the need to start moving back. It was the loss of the
sun to hide his expression and the sudden awareness of his
physical presence that intimated her.

He was dressed in much the same way that she was, in
casual trousers and a plain tee shirt. But it wasn't clothes
that made the man inside them. It wasn't designer labels
or that air of subtle wealth he carried with him that made
her insides draw tightly inwards in sheer self-defence.

She was too vulnerable to him, she realised helplessly.
Too easily diverted by things that held no place in this
room.

'He's gone home,' he told her. 'To England,' he added
almost reluctantly.

'Home? England?' She repeated stupidly. 'But he can't
do that!' she cried. 'He isn't well enough to travel! I need
to see him!'

Luiz took another couple of steps towards her as she
spun round in a full circle so her dazed eyes could check
the room out again, as if she expected him to miraculously
appear and prove Luiz wrong.

But her father didn't appear. And as she made herself
look back at Luiz the sickly suspicion that this was just
another part of his overall plan, to separate father from
daughter, began to take a firm grip. 'You've sent him
away,' she breathed.

'He's gone home to put his house in order,' Luiz sombrely replied.

But she shook her head. 'You made him go so we can't
get together and spoil your plans by coming up with an
alternative solution to our problems.'

'Is there an alternative?'

Gently put, smooth as silk, the question pierced her like
the lethal prick from a scorpion's tail. 'Then why has he
gone?' she demanded, her heart beating so fast that she
could hear it hammering inside her head.

'Guilt,' he told her bluntly. 'He couldn't face you, so he left before you could get here...'

Deserted her, he meant. Ran away, he meant. Left her here to face the rotten music alone, he meant!

It was too much. She couldn't bear it. She turned to leave, but not quickly enough to hide from Luiz the flood of hurt tears that burst into being. His hand snaked out, caught her shoulder, stopping her from walking away.

'Try to understand,' he murmured huskily. 'He saw himself last night for perhaps the first time. He saw the mess he had made of his life—the misery he had made of yours!'

'So he ran,' she mocked. 'How brave of him!'

'It was for the best, Caroline,' Luiz insisted. 'He wants to put his own house in order. Don't condemn him for at least wanting to try before he can bring himself to face you again.'

'In that case, let him swing for his own wretched debts!' she responded in swift and bitter retaliation. 'Find someone else to marry you, Luiz!' she flashed. 'Because I am now taking myself out of it!'

With an angry shrug she tried to free her imprisoned shoulder. All that happened was that the hand turned into a grip of steel.

'I am still *paying* for him to put his house in order,' Luiz inserted with deadly precision.

Caroline sucked in some air, held onto it for as long as she could, then let it go again with such violence that it escaped as a sob. 'So am I, it seems,' she whispered then.

'It is what we agreed,' Luiz confirmed.

And in her mind's eye she had an image of her father, running away like a frightened rabbit while Luiz stood viewing his departure from his lofty position in his eagle's nest, happy to let one tasty meal go because he still had another set cleanly in his sights.

Then she shuddered, and stopped thinking right there, because she just didn't want to know how she was going to describe herself. But still the apt description of a lamb being led meekly to the slaughter managed to fill her head.

And if cynicism could be measured in fathoms, then Caroline knew she was now plunging the very depths as she made herself turn to face him.

'Do you ever lose, Luiz?' she asked him.

His grim mouth flexed on a twist of a smile. 'Very rarely,' he answered honestly.

She nodded, and left it at that. After all, what was there left to say? She was here because Luiz wanted her here. Her father had gone because Luiz had wanted him gone.

'So what happens now?' she asked eventually, knowing the question told him that she was right back on track— just as Luiz wanted.

'Now?' he said curiously, his dark eyes fixed on her beautiful but cold amethyst eyes set in an equally beautiful but coldly composed face. And the twist to his mouth became more pronounced. 'This is what we do, right here and now,' he drawled—and with only that outwardly innocent warning he caught her by the chin, pulled her face up towards him then kissed her—hard.

She just hadn't expected it, so the rush of heat that attacked her nerve-ends had taken tight hold of her before she managed to find the will to pull away. Luiz let her go, but only because he was willing to do so, she was sure of that.

And still smiling that twisted smile, even though he had just used that wretched mouth to kiss her utterly senseless, he tapped one of her burning cheeks with a taunting finger. 'Now that's warmed you up nicely,' he noted smoothly.

She wanted to hit him. He knew she wanted to hit him. Standing there toe to toe, breast-tips to muscle-padded chest, he held her furious eyes with devilishly mocking ones and just dared her to do it!

It was a skin-blistering few moments. Neither moved, neither spoke, neither seemed even to breathe. Tension gnawed and antagonism pulsed—along with a slice of something else that further infuriated her.

Sex was its name. Hot sex, tight sex. Sex that plucked at the angry senses until they sang like an out-of-tune violin. And suddenly she could feel the fine lining of her body begin to ripple in an agonising parody of what happened when he was buried inside her. It wasn't fair. Her senses had no right to betray her like this! It wasn't fair that her breasts were stinging, their tender tips tightening into hard, tight, eager nubs against his wretched breastbone.

'Marriage to you is going to be one hell of an adventure,' he murmured—and effectively brought her tumbling back down to earth with a resounding bump.

She should have shattered. She would have preferred to shatter rather than have to continue to stand here knowing that he knew exactly—and in detail—what she had been feeling.

'I hate you,' she whispered, and spun her back to him with the intention of stalking stiffly away. But her exit was ruined by the sudden appearance of the doctor, Luiz's uncle Fidel.

'Oh,' he said, looking much as Caroline must have looked when she'd first walked in the room. 'Your father has left already?' he asked.

'There was a spare seat on a flight to London he didn't want to miss,' Luiz informed him. 'He has business that needs his immediate attention if he wants to be back here in time for our wedding next week.'

Next week? Caroline tensed. Long fingers came to clasp

her shoulders in a physical warning for her to watch what she said.

'I pray you will both survive till then,' his uncle said sagely. 'If you are to eat at the castle, Luiz, then make sure you take a food-taster with you. For if Consuela could have her wish it would be to see you six feet under the soil rather than have to watch you take what is left of her life away.'

Caroline didn't understand a single word of what was being said. Except that she and Luiz were, it seemed, to be married in a week!

'Don't worry about your father, child,' Fidel said smilingly, obviously reading her expression as one of anxiety for her father. 'He was fighting fit when I saw him this morning. And he will not forget to take his medication again after experiencing the shock he had last night.'

The doctor's beeper began sounding then, cutting short any more discussion other than for him to step up and give Caroline's cheek an affectionate peck before turning briskly away with, 'See you both at the church, God willing!'

Then he was gone, scooting away as abruptly as he had arrived.

'What did he mean, you need a food-taster?' she asked in his uncle's wake. 'And what castle—what wedding?'

'The wedding you should have been expecting,' Luiz drawled. 'The castle is the one I inherited along with my illustrious title. And the food-tasting quip was a joke— though not a very funny joke, I will admit,' he conceded.

It hadn't sounded like a joke to Caroline. In fact it had sounded like a bit of very serious advice! 'I wish you would tell me what is really going on here,' she bit out angrily.

'Feuds and fortunes,' Luiz replied laconically, and halted any further discussion by leading her out into a

PLAY "LUCKY 7" AND GET
THREE FREE GIFTS!

HOW TO PLAY:

1. With a coin, carefully scratch off the silver box at the right. Then check the claim ch[...]
see what we have for you — **2 FREE BOOKS** and a gift — **ALL YOURS! ALL FRE[...]**

2. Send back this card and you'll receive two brand-new Harlequin Presents® novels. [...]
books have a cover price of $3.99 each in the U.S. and $4.50 each in Canada, but the[...]
yours to keep absolutely free.

3. There's no catch. You're [...]
no obligation to buy anything[...]
charge nothing — ZERO — [...]
your first shipment. And you [...]
have to make any minimum nu[...]
of purchases — not even one [...]

4. The fact is thousands of readers enjoy receiving their books by mail from the Harl[...]
Reader Service®. They enjoy the convenience of home delivery...they like getting the[...]
new novels at discount prices, BEFORE they're available in stores...and they love their [...]
to Heart newsletter featuring author news, horoscopes, recipes, book reviews and much [...]

5. We hope that after receiving your free books you'll want to remain a subscriber[...]
the choice is yours — to continue or cancel, any time at all! So why not take us up o[...]
invitation, with no risk of any kind. You'll be glad you did!

YOURS FREE!

PLAY LUCKY 7 FOR THIS EXCITING FREE GIFT!

THIS SURPRISE MYSTERY GIFT COULD BE YOURS FREE WHEN YOU PLAY
LUCKY 7!

Visit us online at
www.eHarlequin.com

The Harlequin Reader Service® — Here's how it works:

BUSINESS REPLY MAIL
FIRST-CLASS MAIL   PERMIT NO. 717   BUFFALO, NY

POSTAGE WILL BE PAID BY ADDRESSEE

HARLEQUIN READER SERVICE
3010 WALDEN AVE
PO BOX 1867
BUFFALO NY 14240-9952

NO POSTAGE
NECESSARY
IF MAILED
IN THE
UNITED STATES

corridor that had too many other people walking about to allow for private conversation.

Vito Martinez was standing by the car waiting for them as they came outside. 'Any messages?' was Luiz's instant enquiry as they approached him.

'Nothing that can't wait,' the other man answered with a telling glance in Caroline's direction.

It niggled her to catch that glance. Just as a lot of other things were now niggling her. 'You two should think about joining the Secret Service,' she snapped out tartly, and climbed into the back of the car without waiting for a response.

A few seconds went by before Luiz eventually joined her. Car doors slammed, the engine fired and behind his protective shield of glass Vito Martinez set them all into smooth motion.

'Vito meant no offence,' Luiz said quietly.

Caroline twisted her head to show him amethyst eyes turned smoky grey with anger. 'Tell me, is that Vito the croupier, Vito the waiter, or Vito the chauffeur you are talking about?' she asked sarcastically.

'It is Vito my security chief and most trusted employee,' he replied very levelly, but it was a silken warning to watch her tongue.

Caroline was feeling too fed up with the whole darn situation to watch her tongue. 'Oh, I see, Mr Versatility, then,' she mocked. 'Does that mean he's the one that pulls out the toenails of your enemies for you in between making sure that sick old men catch flights out of a country you don't want them to be in?'

'Vito did not chauffeur your father to the airport; he chauffeured you to the hospital, if you recall.'

'Ah, he has assistants, then.' She nodded understandingly.

The steady gaze hardened fractionally. 'You, I think, are gunning for a fight.'

He was right; she was.

Luiz's eyes narrowed. 'Be very—very careful, *querida*,' he warned.

'Stop the car,' she demanded.

Why she said it Caroline certainly didn't know—but without hesitation Luiz leant forward and pressed a switch that sent the glass sliding downwards.

'Stop the car, Vito,' he commanded. The car came to a smooth halt.

Caroline was out on the side of the road before she'd had a chance to realise she was there. It was crazy. The whole situation was crazy! She didn't know what she was doing here in Marbella! She didn't know what she was doing letting Luiz Vazquez control her life! And she certainly didn't know what she was doing standing here looking out over the Bay of Malaga beneath a burning hot summer sun—shivering like a block of ice!

She heard Luiz's feet scrape on loose tarmac but didn't turn around. She felt his closeness when he came to stand behind her but didn't acknowledge he was there. Her eyes were hurting, and so was her head. And, lower down, that band of steel was encasing her chest again.

'In the hours since we met, you've tricked me, blackmailed me, kidnapped me and seduced me,' she told him in a tight little voice. 'You've helped me put my father into hospital, then had him neatly spirited away. In short, you've layered shock after shock after shock on me, in some neatly worked out little sequence aimed, I think, to keep me constantly knocked off balance. And you know what, Luiz?'

'What?' he prompted.

'I haven't got a single shred of an idea as to *why* you've decided to do this to me!'

He didn't reply—had she really expected him to? Caroline asked herself bitterly as she swung round to look directly at him. His lean hard face was giving nothing away—as usual. And as she stood there, letting the silence stretch between them in the hopes that it would force an explanation out of him, she found her mind scanning back to their seven-week romance seven years ago, looking for clues as to why he was treating her like this.

But the only thing she could come up with was the ugly scene they had had on the night she'd left Marbella for good. Luiz had been standing there, much as he was now, tall and tense, while she'd flung accusation after accusation at him.

'How could you do it, Luiz?' she could hear herself sobbing. 'How could you take everything I had to offer you then leave my arms to go and win money from my father in the casino night after night?'

'I don't suppose it has occurred to you that it was your father who was trying to win money from me?' he'd bitten back coldly.

His attempt to shift the blame to her father had only infuriated her more. '*You're* the professional!' she'd cried. 'You told me yourself that you used to make a living from gambling—whereas my father is just a gullible fool!'

'He's an *addict*, Caroline,' Luiz had hit back brutally. 'A compulsive gambler who is therefore willing to play *anyone* so long as he plays!'

'Well, he says he played you,' she'd told him. 'Are you telling me that he lied?'

'No,' he'd said heavily. 'He didn't lie.'

It had been the death of a beautiful love affair, she recalled as she came swimming back to the present. She had walked away. Luiz had let her go. And not a single day had gone by since when she hadn't closed her eyes and seen his ice-cold expression as she'd left him standing there—and wished more than anything that things could have been different.

'This has nothing to do with the past, but with the future.'

Luiz spoke so suddenly that she had to blink a couple of times before she could realise that he was actually answering the question she'd put to him before she'd gone floating off into memories.

'I need a wife to secure the final part of my inheritance,' he explained. 'And, having come to terms with the fact that I have to have one, I have decided that I would prefer that wife to be you. Does that make you feel any better?' he taunted lazily.

No, it didn't. She went pale. 'I'm just a convenient means to an end, then,' she said, seeing just how *conveniently* vulnerable to persuasion she had been for him. He hadn't even had to woo her, just make her an offer she couldn't refuse.

'As I am to you,' he pointed out coldly. 'Which seems pretty fair all the way round, don't you think?'

She found herself stumped for an argument because, put like that, he was right! Luiz waited, though, ruthless devil until he was sure she was not going to throw him yet another tantrum on some other quickly thought up charge.

Then, 'Can we go now?' he requested, oh, so sardonically. 'Only I have a lot of things to do before we leave here in the morning.'

Leave...

He was doing it again! Knocking her off balance with yet another one of his little surprises! 'Leave for where?' she gasped out.

'Cordoba,' he replied, then turned on his heel and strode back to the car.

Caroline followed—did she really have any choice? she

angrily mocked herself. 'What's in Cordoba?' she demanded, the moment she was back inside the car.

'A small valley in the mountains that goes by the name of Valle de los Angeles,' he explained as the car began to accelerate. 'And there in the valley stands the Castillo de los Angeles, which belongs to Luiz Angeles de Vazquez, Conde del Valle de los Angeles...'

And if she thought she'd plumbed the depths of cynicism in her own way a while back, then Luiz was now demonstrating what little she knew about cynicism at all.

'There, *el conde*,' he continued in the same nerve-wincing tone, 'will wed his betrothed in the church of the Valle de los Angeles, as is tradition for all condes del Valle de los Angeles. Then he will carry his bride off to his impressive *castillo*—just in time to banish the resident wicked witch before he ravishes his new Condesa.'

'Wicked witch?' she quizzed, picking out the only part in the acutely sarcastic agenda that managed to completely baffle her.

'*Sí.*' He nodded. 'Doña Consuela Engracia de Vazquez—the present Condesa del Valle de los Angeles.'

'The lady your uncle mentioned earlier,' she remembered.

'*Sí,*' he said again. 'Tío Fidel is a very shrewd man,' he allowed. 'He is also the only member of my family that you can safely trust,' he then added, more seriously. 'It will be wise of yōu, *querida,* to mark that I said that...'

CHAPTER SEVEN

MARK it, he'd said...

But twenty-four hours later it was Luiz who seemed to be marking what he'd said, Caroline noted, as the closer they got to Cordoba, the more uptight he became.

Sitting beside him, she stared at the forever-changing vista beyond the car window and wondered what it was that was eating into him today. He should be happy, she mused testily. After all, he'd got himself one very meek and obedient passenger here, who hadn't put up a single protest against his arrogant take-over of her life—well, not since her performance out on the Marbella road yesterday, anyway.

But then she hadn't been given the opportunity to protest about anything else, she reminded herself. Because as soon as he'd delivered her back to his villa Luiz had shot off again with his security chief, and she hadn't set eyes on him until he'd come to collect her for this journey this morning.

And he had arrived dressed for travelling, in a light-weight black linen suit and white shirt, looking almost as uptight as he did right now!

'Are you ready? Is that your case? Do you think we can go, then?' Terse to the point of rudeness, he had barely given her chance to reply. And other than for a quick down and away glance at the dusky mauve skinny top and cream tailored skirt she had chosen to wear for the journey, not once had he allowed himself to make full eye contact with her.

Because he'd known that to do so would give her an

invitation to start speaking her mind again. Something Luiz obviously didn't want. Something Luiz obviously *still* didn't want, since he'd maintained that barrier throughout the whole time they had been travelling.

Maybe he was afraid she was going to start demanding to know where he had spent last night, she mused with an acidity that stung in her blood. Because he certainly hadn't spent it with her, in his own bed. And he might be refusing to look at her, but she had certainly looked at him enough to notice the signs of a man who hadn't got much sleep!

She had, she recalled smugly. She'd slept like a baby and hadn't even missed him until she'd woken up this morning to find the place beside her was still as smooth as it had been when she'd fallen asleep!

Liar, a tiny voice in her head said. You woke several times and worried because he wasn't there. You missed him too! Which makes the lie all that more pathetic!

'Damn,' Luiz muttered, bringing the car to a sudden stop. 'I think we just missed the turning…'

Slamming the car into reverse gear, he began driving them back the way they had just come, past a junction sporting a road sign indicating that a place called Los Aminos was off to the left.

He stopped the car again, uttered an irritated sigh and reached for the glove compartment to extract a road map, which he then spread out across the steering wheel and began to frown at.

Caroline frowned too. 'Don't you *know* where we're going?'

'No,' he replied.

Blunt and gruff, it didn't really encourage more questioning. But she was confused. It didn't seem likely, knowing his gift of near photo-perfect memory, that he could have actually got them lost!

'How often have you made this journey?' she asked
condescension feathering her tone.

A long index finger was following the wavy red line
that cut a path through from Marbella to Cordoba. A sudden vision of that same finger tracing circles around her
navel sent an injection of heat directly to her thighs. It was
shameful. She despised herself.

'I haven't,' Luiz said.

It took a moment for her to take that answer in. Then
she noticed that the finger had stopped at a road junction.
This road junction, Caroline supposed, glancing up at the
sign, then back at the map to see that indeed the finger
was touching this precise point on the map.

'You mean you haven't done it from Marbella before?'
she finally decided.

The finger began moving again, mesmerising her when
she knew she shouldn't let it, as it traced a line off to the
left that went skirting around Cordoba.

'I meant I have not been there—period,' he clarified,
bringing the finger to a stop at a tiny dot on the map that
bore the name Valle de los Angeles.

The remark came as such a surprise that it had her turning in her seat to stare at his grimly taut profile. 'Why
not?' she demanded.

He didn't answer. Instead he began neatly folding up
the map again, and just let the silence fill with the same
tension they had been travelling with before he'd lost his
sense of direction.

'Luiz?' she prompted.

'Because I knew I wouldn't be welcome, okay?' he
launched at her tightly.

'But it belongs to you!' she exclaimed.

'What does that have to do with being made welcome?'
Leaning across her, he put the map back into the glove
compartment.

Sudden enlightenment hit. 'The one who might poison you,' she murmured softly. 'The resident wicked witch—your father's widow?'

'You bet,' he replied, shifting the car into gear.

'And she—resents you?' She tried to put it kindly, but still Luiz released a scornful laugh.

'Wouldn't you resent the man who has usurped your own son's position in the family?'

His father had *another* son? Luiz had a half-brother? While she sat there absorbing this latest piece of news, Luiz spun the steering wheel and set them moving into the left-hand fork in the road. A long and dusty winding road lay ahead of them. With a surge of power Luiz accelerated along it. Top-of-the-range plush as the car was, custom-built for quality performance with optimum comfort as it was, the BMW could do nothing about the kind of atmosphere its occupants created for themselves. It proceeded to throb with a hundred questions one of them wanted to ask, mingling with answers the other was clearly reluctant to provide.

In the end Caroline plumped for the most pressing question. 'Why you instead of him?' she queried.

'Because I am the bastard and he is not?' Luiz mockingly questioned the question.

Caroline flushed slightly at his blunt candour. Luiz might be possessive of his privacy now, but he had not been seven years ago. He had been very open then about his life as a fatherless child, living in a run-down tenement in the backstreets of New York with a mother who had struggled to make ends meet. She knew his mother had died when he was only nine years old and that Luiz had lived out the rest of his childhood in a state institution.

'I was chosen because I possess a lot of individual wealth and the family itself is practically bankrupt.'

In other words, his father had named Luiz as his successor out of expediency rather than desire, she realised. It was no wonder Luiz sounded so bitter and cynical about the whole thing.

'And your half-brother and his mother?' she asked. 'Where does it leave them in all of this?'

If it was at all possible, his expression turned even harder. 'Out in the cold, as far as I am concerned. As they have kept me out in the cold for most of my life.'

No wonder he had left it so long without bothering to go and meet his inheritance face on, she grimly concluded. For Luiz was not a fool; he knew what he was going to find waiting for him. Which left begging just one more question she couldn't leave unasked.

'Our marriage?' she prompted. 'What has it to do with all of this?'

For a moment she thought he wasn't going to answer. His mouth was tight, his eyes shot through with a hard glitter as they followed the snaking line of the road ahead. Then, 'Our marriage is the means by which I put them in the cold,' he replied. 'For by my father's decree they may continue to live in the castle only until I marry.'

His ruthless streak was showing again. And Caroline was beginning to feel sorry for Luiz's new-found family. She had a horrible feeling they had no idea what kind of man it was who was coming to meet them today, or they would have packed their bags and got out before he arrived.

'Ever heard of the word forgiveness?' she advanced huskily.

'Forgiveness is usually only given to those that want it,' he replied.

Slick and shrewd though his reply was, it still made her shiver. She fell silent after that. And they didn't speak again throughout the miles they ate up until they entered the sleepy little village of Los Aminos.

'We'll stop here for some lunch,' Luiz decided.

Caroline didn't demur. She was beginning to feel stiff and thirsty, and a break for lunch was a preferable option to keeping on driving towards she knew not what.

Luiz found a little café with wooden tables set outside beneath a faded blue awning. Pulling into the kerb, he climbed out of the car, then stood stretching taut muscles while he waited for Caroline to join him. The inn wasn't what you would call a fashionable place, but the basket of bread and bowl of crisp salad they were served were fresh and tasty.

She asked for a Coke, and Luiz did the same, then they sat sharing the lunch between them as if they did this kind of thing all the time. But the silence was still there, pulsing between them.

Reaching for another thick chunk of bread, she asked, 'How much further?' in an effort to break the deadlock.

'Same again,' Luiz answered briefly, while reaching for some more bread himself.

She huffed out a weary sigh that turned into a yawn. The day was hot and the air was humid, and she had lied about sleeping well last night, so now she was beginning to feel the dragging effects of hardly any sleep at all.

'Tired?' Luiz asked.

'It's the heat,' she blamed. 'And the travelling. Where did you sleep last night?'

And she could have bitten off her tongue the moment she caught the sudden gleam in his eyes. 'Missed me, did you?' he murmured silkily.

'No,' she denied. 'I slept like a log.'

'Well, I missed you,' he told her huskily.

Warily she glanced up, thinking he was just teasing— but he wasn't. And the atmosphere between them suddenly took a violent change. He was looking at her as if he was seeing her sitting there naked.

She looked away again quickly—but not quickly enough to stop her insides from coiling tightly, and she could feel a sensual tingling between her thighs.

'We could go somewhere,' Luiz suggested.

Caroline almost choked on her bread. Was he saying what she thought he was saying? She picked up her Coke and gulped at it in an effort to disperse the bread.

'You only have to say yes...'

Oh, for goodness' sake! she thought. 'No, Luiz!' she whispered hoarsely. And made the mistake of looking into his eyes again.

They were on fire. He wanted her. And he wanted her now! 'Stop it,' she breathed, feeling her cheeks begin to glow, and sent trembling fingers on a wild foray of the salad bowl—only to meet his fingers halfway, because he was reaching for her.

It was like making contact with a high-voltage cable. Caroline snatched her hand away on a sharp gasp; Luiz did more than that—he released a low, short, explicit curse, then lurched angrily to his feet.

It a state of near shock, because she didn't know what had happened between them, she watched him dig into his pocket for some money and toss it onto the table before reaching out to grab her hand.

And this time there was no snatching it back as if the contact was too electrifying to tolerate because Luiz wasn't letting go. He turned and began striding off down the sun-drenched and dusty street, trailing her behind him like some recalcitrant child he was taking off to be smacked.

She wanted to protest—demand where he thought he was going, when the car was parked the other way! But the sheer ferocity etched into his lean face was enough to keep the words locked up tight in her throat.

Suddenly he stopped dead, tightened his grip on her

hand and turned to walk her inside the foyer to what turned out to be a small hotel.

'Luiz—no!' she managed to gasp out at last, when the disturbing suspicion of what he was intending began to take horrifying shape in her head.

He completely ignored her. It was as if the devil was driving him. His face was taut, his jaw set, and she felt her cheeks suffuse with hot self-conscious colour as he grimly began negotiating the price of the hotel's best suite—on an hourly basis.

It was awful, the most embarrassing situation she had ever experienced in her life! The concierge kept on sending her brief but knowing little glances, and she didn't know where to put herself as Luiz placed a wad of notes on the desk, scrawled his signature in the register, then accepted the key the concierge was holding out to him before turning towards the stairs.

'I can't believe you're doing this!' Caroline choked out as he began striding upwards, pulling her with him.

He didn't even bother to answer, his expression so fierce that she began to quail inside her shoes as he led her along a narrow landing then unlocked a door and swung her inside.

The hotel was small and very simple; the room—darkened by closed shutters over the window—was nothing more than a bed, a table and a couple of chairs set on floorboards, and there was no air conditioning to help take away the suffocating heat. But by the time he had closed the door behind them she couldn't have cared less what the room was like. She was out of breath, feeling a nerve-tingling excitement that didn't go down well with how she knew she should be feeling in a situation like this!

'What the hell has got into you?' she demanded, managing to get her hand free at last.

Again he didn't answer, but then he didn't really need

to, because she knew what had *got into* him. In fact it was written all over his hard-boned, muscle-locked face!

With a growing sense of awareness she stepped warily away from him, only to watch in a kind of wide-eyed fascination as he shrugged out of his jacket and tossed it aside, then began pulling his shirt off over his head.

The two items landed on a chair. His bronzed torso expanded, then relaxed, as if removing those garments had been a matter of life or death.

Fire and ice, she found herself likening, as she waited breathlessly to discover what was going to come next. The fire was in his passion, the ice the medium he used to keep the other suppressed. It was a dynamic combination, one that set some secret engine she hadn't known she possessed humming throughout her entire system. She had never experienced anything like it. But it held her completely captivated as she watched the passion melt its way through the ice until all that was left was a blistering intent that began scorching her flesh.

'Luiz, this isn't—' Funny, she had been going to say, but he reached for her, caught her wrists and used them to draw her body against him, then fed them around his neck.

Burning eyes became hidden beneath sweeping lashes as he lowered his gaze to where his fingers began to undo the tiny buttons down the front of her top.

It was all so intense, so very macho that she didn't know whether she was feeling fiercely excited by it or just plain scared. But she didn't attempt to get away from him—which was an answer, she supposed. And as his hands brushed the top aside, to reveal the flimsy thin silk bra beneath, her spine arched slightly in feline invitation for him to touch what he had uncovered. Yet when he did touch her he did it in a way that completely snagged her breath. Because it was not the sensually possessive caress she had been expecting. His hands simply needed to touch her like this.

'Why?' she whispered. She just didn't understand this man one iota. He could be so cold, so utterly ruthless with his demands. But this was different. This was—compulsion.

'I need you,' was all he said. Then his mouth was crushing hers apart, and nothing else seemed to matter after that. Their clothes disappeared in hurried succession, their flesh coming together in an intoxicating mix of hunger, heat and sweat.

The bed waited, and as they folded down onto its soft mattress the smell of freshly starched linen came wafting cleanly round them. It was a smell that seemed to make it all perfect, somehow, though Caroline didn't know why it should.

As time made deep and sensual inroads into the afternoon, without them being aware of it passing, they forget where they were supposed to be going—or maybe they chose to forget. It didn't seem to matter. It was hot and it was steamy and it was a much more appealing journey, one that explored the senses to the exclusion of none, allowed no room for inhibition. It pretended that this was good and right and absolutely the only thing in the world either of them should be doing.

So they made love all afternoon, slept a little in an intimate tangle of limbs, before rousing to begin making love all over again.

'Why, Luiz?' she dared to ask him again, when they'd quietened. 'Why are we here like this?'

'You're always asking me *why*,' he complained, nuzzling his mouth against her throat.

'Only because you keep hitting me with the unexpected,' she told him.

'Well, I thought the answer this time should be obvious,'

he said with a grimace. 'You're so beautiful you make me ache,' he murmured deeply. 'And so damn desirable that I can't even control myself long enough to get us from one place to another without having to stop off in the middle of the journey to do—this…'

His mouth took hers in the kind of kiss that sent any further words spinning off into oblivion. But she knew that, no matter how good for her ego his answer had been, it wasn't the real reason why they had ended up here in this bed, making love like this.

She had triggered something back at the lunch table when she had given away the fact that she'd missed him in her bed last night. She only wished she could understand what that something was, because then maybe she could begin to understand Luiz.

Eventually they reluctantly decided that they should be moving if they wanted to reach their destination before dark. Caroline went off to shower in the tiny bathroom they had discovered down the corridor. When she came back it was to find that the sun had left this side of the building and Luiz had opened the shutters and the windows to allow some warm but fresher air to filter into the room.

He was standing over a small breakfast-type table on which, she was surprised to find, rested a wooden tray with what looked like a plate of sandwiches and a tall jug full of iced water.

'Mmm, the hotelier in action, I see,' she remarked lightly.

He glanced round, grimaced a smile at her, then turned back to the two tall tumblers he was in the process of filling. 'We didn't really do lunch justice,' he said. 'And, knowing the Spanish habit of eating late in the evening, I thought we might as well have a snack before we leave.'

The ice chinked as it fell from jug to tumbler, and drew

her across the room. She hadn't realised she was feeling so thirsty until she heard that irresistible sound.

'Thank you,' she said, accepting a glass from him.

'The sandwiches are only cheese and ham, but help yourself,' he invited—then turned to go and take his turn in the bathroom, leaving Caroline to gulp thirstily at the water as she took another interested look around her.

What had only been quite seductively mystical shadows in the room before had now taken on rather interesting shapes with the light streaming in. The pale green painted walls wore the patina of age, and the polished floor had thick hand-made rugs thrown upon it. The bed was one of those big old heavy things you had to hitch yourself up to sit upon, and the two bedside cabinets had a pair of matching table lamps on them that would probably fetch a tidy sum in today's post-war collectors' market.

Which was her professional head talking, she acknowledged with a wry smile as she chose a sandwich then sat down in one of the two leather club chairs that flanked the little table. For she liked the two lamps exactly where they were, so to start thinking of how much they would fetch at auction, only to be carried off elsewhere, was not where she wanted her mind to go right now.

In fact she liked the whole room in general, and was aware, when she thought that, why she did. This room would always stay in her memory as the place where she finally found peace with her own feelings for Luiz. She loved him, she wanted him, she needed to be with him, no matter how he'd used her in the past or was using her now, in the present.

And if Luiz never came to love her back, at least she knew without a single doubt that he wanted her—passionately. She could live with that. She could *build* on that.

He arrived back in the room freshly showered and

dressed again, and her stomach gave a soft curling quiver in recognition of the way she was feeling about him now.

Picking up a sandwich, he took the other chair and folded his long frame into it. 'Not quite a palace,' he drawled, glancing round them.

'Nice, though.' She smiled. 'I like little out-of-the way places like this.'

'As opposed to five-star air conditioned luxury?' he mocked.

She nodded, still smiling. 'This place has soul,' she explained. 'It has secrets hidden in its darkest closets.' Not to mention my own secret, she mused ruefully. 'It has stories to tell of things long ago. These chairs, for instance,' she said, reaching for her tumbler. 'Who sat in them first? Who spilled their pot of ink on this wonderful table?' she pondered, stroking a loving finger over the black stain. 'Was it a woman? Was she writing a farewell note to her secret lover, so blinded by her own tears that she knocked the pot over? Or was it a man?' she then suggested, her eyes darkening subtly as she wove stories in a way her father would have recognised, because she had always done it. But for Luiz this was new, and it held him riveted as he watched her softened face and listened to her dreamy voice. 'Was he so engrossed in writing his one big novel that he spilled the ink in distraction?'

'Both things could happen just as easily in a five-star hotel,' Luiz pointed out dryly.

But Caroline shook her head. 'If this table had had ink spilled on it in one of your hotels it would have been replaced with a nice new one before you had a chance to blink. No soul in that, Luiz,' she told him sagely. 'No soul at all.'

'So you like all things old and preferably flawed.' He smiled. 'Is that what you're saying?'

'I like *some* things old and *sometimes* flawed,' she

amended. 'I also like new, so long as it tells a story. I like *interesting*,' she decided that said it best.

'Well, I think I can probably promise you *interesting* where we are going,' he said.

And suddenly the cynicism was back. Impulsively Caroline reached for his hand across the table. 'Don't, Luiz,' she pleaded. 'Don't spoil it.'

He glanced down to where her hand covered his. His expression remained cast in stone for a while, then he released a small sigh, turning his hand to capture hers, and got to his feet, pulling her up with him.

His mouth was gentle on hers—seeming to be offering an apology. But when she made a move to deepen the kiss he withdrew, and his expression was still closed when he said, 'We really have to be going.'

The afternoon of near perfect harmony, she realised, was over…

CHAPTER EIGHT

LEAVING Los Aminos behind, they began another twen
miles or so of driving before they would reach their de
tination. As the car ate up the miles so the scene
changed, from sprawling plains into rolling hills at fir
then eventually into a more rugged terrain, where the hi
took on the shape of forest-covered mountains.

The quality of the road they were travelling on chang
also, narrowing to little more than a single car width as
wound them upwards on a steep climb that hugged
mountain face on one side and left sheer drops into de
ravines exposed on the other.

'How much further?' Caroline asked, beginning to fe
as if they had been climbing for ever.

'The next valley,' Luiz replied. And his tension w
back, in the clenched jawbone, the white-knuckled han
gripping the steering wheel.

He didn't want to come here, she silently reiterated. I
didn't want to be this person who had to meet with peop
who were already programmed to hate and resent him.

And there was a hint of ill-omen in the way the air
the mountain suddenly turned colder, raising goosebum
on her arms she rubbed at with a small shiver.

Instantly Luiz touched a switch that changed the air co
ditioning from cold to warm. 'You should have brought
sweater,' he said.

'If I'd known where we were coming, perhaps I mig
have thought of that myself,' she smiled ruefully.

'There's a car rug on the back seat if you—'

'I'm fine,' she softly assured him, wishing she could s

116

the same about Luiz. But he was far from fine, she observed worriedly. For the higher they climbed the more tense he became.

'You could always make the grand gesture and pass everything over to your half-brother then just walk away,' she gently suggested.

His dark head shook. 'That isn't an option,' he stated.

'Because you feel he owes you for the years you had nothing while he had everything?' she posed.

'Because it just isn't an option,' he repeated in a tight voice that warned her that she was prodding what was really a very dangerous animal, the way he was feeling right now.

On a sigh, she took the hint, and fell silent. They were driving between the tall peaks of two mountains now, still hugging the side of one while the other stood guard in the distance. And really, Caroline observed, if they didn't reach the valley soon then the only place left for them to go would be off the side of the mountain, because surely they couldn't climb any higher?

Then—without warning—it finally happened. They rounded a deep bend, suddenly found themselves driving through a split in the mountain—and there it was.

The most beautiful place Caroline had ever seen in her entire life.

'Oh, Luiz,' she breathed, while he seemed to freeze for a couple of taut seconds, before bringing the car to a stop.

After that they both sat there and just stared in breathless awe at what had opened up in front of them.

The Valle de los Angeles... It could not possibly be anything else, Caroline decided. And they'd caught it at probably one of its most perfect moments, with the late sun pouring fire down its lush green slopes to brush everything on the wide valley bottom with a touch of sheer magic.

Directly below them blushing white-painted building stood clustered around a tiny church sitting in the cent of the village square. From there, and running parallel wit the valley, snaked a gentle stream with a narrow dirt roa running beside it through line upon line of what looke like fruit trees planted in uniform rows.

And there, standing out like the place from which a fairytales were conceived, stood a white-walled, red-roofe castle, complete with battlements and cylindrical tower and even a drawbridge beneath which the stream ran whi the dirt road stopped in front of it.

'This is perfection,' Caroline whispered.

Luiz stiffened sharply, as if the sound of her voice ha woken him from a daze. But he said not a word—not single word. He just put the car into gear and set the moving again—with a whole new level of tension sizzli around him that kept Caroline's tongue still.

Going down into the valley was not as hair-raising as had been climbing up to it. Instead of teeth-tingling she drops on one side they were zigzagging down through series of carefully cultivated terraces that spread out c either side of them. It was all so lush and green and ol viously fertile that it was no surprise to find herself reco nising just about every fruit-bearing shrub and plant ima inable growing here.

The road eventually brought them out in the valley bo tom, just behind the village. Driving through the villa itself was another experience entirely. People were o strolling or just chatting to their neighbours, while do barked around the feet of playing children. It was like e tering another world. Nothing about the place seemed qui real. Not the dark-eyed, dark-haired simply dressed peop or their immaculate white homes with their brightly cc oured painted doors and shutters.

And the sense of unreality deepened when everyone went still and stared as they drove by.

Oh, my, Caroline thought, they know who we are! Or at least, she amended that, they know who Luiz is. And she felt the hairs on the back of her neck begin to tingle as she watched them stare curiously in through the sun-tinted car windows at Luiz's stern dark profile.

'Do I start referring to you as *el conde* now?' she asked in a shaky attempt to lighten the tension.

'Try the Vazquez bastard,' Luiz gritted.

And that was the point when she began to lose her patience with him, because while Luiz was busy seeing himself as the Vazquez bastard, he was blinding himself to what these people were seeing when they looked at him.

They were seeing the lean, dark, arrogant profile of one of their own. They were seeing their own black silk hair and olive-tinted skin and dark brown eyes that stated, quite plainly, Here is one of us. Their expressions were not deriding or hostile, or even vaguely contemptuous, they were simply curious.

If anything, it was the glances *she* received that brought other forces to the fore. For what was she to these people? She was a pale-skinned, blonde-haired utter stranger, with eyes the colour of amethysts. Nothing even remotely familiar about the way she looked to them.

When the road opened up into the village square, with the sweet little church in its centre, the people all jumped to attention—except for one young man, who ran across the square then into the church. Mere seconds later, a priest in his simple black robes appeared in the opening. Very tall, very thin, and with a shock of white hair framing his lined face, he watched them pass by with a solemn shrewdness that made Caroline's insides tingle.

'Is this the church where we are expected to marry?' she asked in a choked little voice.

'Yes,' Luiz replied.

'Then don't you think we should have stopped and [at] least passed the time of day with the priest?' It was censu[re] and anxiety rolled into one question, because she didn['t] want to offend these people, and she was sure that on[ce] Luiz had got over whatever it was that was slowly killi[ng] him he wouldn't want to think that he had offended anyo[ne] either.

Luiz shook his head. Not once did he let his eyes dive[rt] from the way ahead as he grimly kept them moving acro[ss] the square and through the next gauntlet of curious spe[c]tators.

He didn't even relax when they left the village and b[e]gan to pass between the neatly tended fruit groves. Oran[ge] groves, lemon groves, peach and apricot groves. 'How c[an] a place like this be bankrupt?' she questioned on a fre[sh] bout of awe. It was all so rich in everything that life cou[ld] offer.

'Through the extravagances of its previous owner[s,]' Luiz informed her cynically.

He had to mean his own father. 'Nobody *owns* som[e]thing like this,' Caroline objected. 'They are merely guar[d]ians, whose responsibility it is to take care of it all duri[ng] their term of office. And if they can't see what an hono[ur] and a privilege that has to be, then they deserve to lo[se] custody.'

'Spoken like a true lady to the manor born,' Luiz d[e]rided. 'Maybe I should just cut my unworthy losses a[nd] sign it all over to you.'

'And you can mock me all you like, *el conde*,' s[he] sniped right back, 'But if you can't grasp the concept [of] what I am saying then maybe you should do just that.'

'Lecture over?' Luiz clipped.

'Yes,' she sighed, wondering wearily why she bother[ed] to take him on like this. The man was impervious to an[y] thing anyone said that didn't suit his own view of things! 'I've finished.'

'Good,' he murmured. 'Because I think we've arrived, and I am beginning to feel like hell...'

As surprise admissions went, that one really managed to strike at the heart of her. She turned in her seat, saw how pale he had gone, saw how clenched his face muscles were and automatically looked where he was looking—and felt everything inside her shudder to a resounding halt.

For while they had been sniping at each other they had come to the end of the fruit groves and driven over the drawbridge, beneath a wide archway cut into the whitewashed wall that surrounded what she supposed must be the castle's private enclave.

She had never, ever seen anything quite like it. From up on the mountain it had all looked pretty stunning, but from down here, on the valley bottom and this close up, the castle was nothing short of enchanting, with its whitewashed walls blushing in the dying sunlight.

It was all so outstandingly—dramatically—beautiful. Even the formally laid out gardens they were now passing through took the breath away. The driveway opened up into a wide cobbled courtyard with a statue of Neptune spouting water into a circular pool, guarding the huge arched entrance into the castle itself.

Luiz stopped the car. Without a word they climbed out, then just stood gazing around.

'It's a folly,' Caroline murmured softly.

'Hmm?' Luiz's dark head swung round to frown a blank look at her.

'The castle,' she explained. 'It's not what it appears to be.'

'What makes you say that?' He seemed to have a struggle to get his voice to work, but once he had spoken some of that awful strain eased from his face.

'Look around you,' she invited. 'There is absolutely no reason for anyone to build a fortified castle down here in the valley. The mountains themselves are the only protection needed down here. If you'd wanted to protect what was yours, you would have built up there, where we came in through the pass in the mountain. This...' she gave a nod of her head towards the castle '...was built to satisfy someone's eccentric ego. A folly,' she repeated, looking frontward again. 'But a beautiful folly...'

And if his family were guilty of bankrupting themselves due to their personal extravagances, she added silently, then at least it had not been at the expense of their exquisite home.

Luiz's home now, she extended, looking across the top of the car at this man who was such a complicated mix of so many different cultures that it was no wonder he kept most of his real self hidden—he probably didn't know who he actually was himself!

'We're being watched,' Luiz murmured.

'Mmm,' Caroline replied. 'I know.' She had felt the eyes piercing her flesh from behind leaded glass windows from the moment they climbed out of the car. 'So, what do you want to do now?' she asked. 'Bang on the door and claim ownership? Or do we take the more civilised approach and wait until we are invited in?'

But even as she put the two lightly mocking suggestions to him the great door behind Neptune was drawing open. Her heart skipped a beat. On the other side of the car she heard Luiz's feet scrape against gravel. Without thinking twice about it, she walked around the car and went to stand beside him.

As she did so a man appeared in the doorway, small, thin and quite old, his expressionless face giving no hint as to whether they were to be made welcome or simply grudgingly allowed to enter the castle's hallowed inner sanctum.

'It looks like it's showtime,' Caroline said softly.

'Looks like it,' Luiz agreed, and although he reached out to catch hold of her hand, as if he needed to feel her presence for moral support, she was relieved to see that the implacable Luiz Vazquez was back in place again and the other, tense and uncomfortable one had been firmly shut away.

Together they walked around the fountain and up to the door. With a slight bow of his dark head, the man murmured, 'Welcome *señor—señorita*,' with absolutely no inflexion in his voice whatsoever. 'If you would kindly come this way?'

The man stepped to one side in an invitation for them to precede him inside, and as the door closed quietly behind them they found themselves standing in a vast hallway built of oak and stone, with an eight-foot-wide solid stone stairway as its main feature. The rough plastered walls were painted in a soft peach colour, adding warmth to what could quite easily appear coldly inhospitable.

Caroline felt her tummy muscles begin to flutter. Beside her, Luiz's fingers tightened their grip on hers. He was used to big reception halls. He was used to standing in beautiful surroundings. But this was different. This was his past meeting head-on with his present. Even she, who had always known the place where her roots were planted, was acutely aware of how significant this moment must be for him.

Yet his voice was smooth and as calm as still water when he turned to speak to the old man. 'And you are?' he enquired, sounding every inch the noble Conde. Considering what she knew he was feeling inside, Caroline was proud of him.

'Pedro, sir. I am the butler here,' the old man replied—

and there was respect in his tone. He for one wasn't con-
demning Luiz for being the Vazquez bastard. 'Please,' he
invited. 'If you will follow me...'

He began leading them across a polished stone floor past
two suits of armour that were guarding the stairs. There
were artefacts scattered about this hall that made
Caroline's head whirl as it went into professional mode.

Maybe Luiz knew it. 'Enough *soul* here for you?' he
questioned lazily.

'Interesting,' she shot back with a smile, then moved a
little closer to his side when Pedro opened a pair of huge
wooden doors and bowed them politely inside.

'Señor Luiz Vazquez and Señorita Newbury,' he announced, to whoever was waiting for them. And Caroline
hadn't missed the fact that the butler had not referred to
Luiz as *el conde* once since they had arrived.

If Luiz noticed the omission, he didn't show it. His expression was relaxed, his grip on Caroline's hand secure,
and his stride was as graceful as always as he strode into
what turned out to be a beautifully appointed drawing
room, with a huge stone fireplace that almost filled one
wall—where a woman stood, awaiting their arrival.

Black-haired, black-eyed, slender and petite, she was
wearing a silver grey silk suit that was as steely-looking
as the expression she was wearing on her face as she stared
directly at Luiz, while he stared coldly back.

For a long, dreadful moment after Pedro had quietly
retired, closing the door behind him, nobody uttered a single word while these two main protagonists studied each
other, and Caroline stood witnessing it happen without taking a single breath.

Then, 'Welcome,' the woman said.

'Tía Consuela,' Luiz replied stiltedly.

Caroline hid the urge to frown. Tía? she was thinking.
Why was Luiz referring to this woman as his *aunt?* Surely

if she was anything to him then she was some kind of stepmother?

'You look like your father,' the woman observed.

'And you have a look of my mother—though you look in much better health than she did when I saw her last.'

Incisive, cold enough to freeze the blood, it was also a puzzle solved for Caroline. This woman was Luiz's mother's sister. It was no wonder his grip was suddenly biting into her fingers. What had gone on here thirty-odd years ago?

Feuds and fortunes, he'd said, she recalled suddenly. And she began to get a sense of what had probably happened, most of it revolving round two sisters, one man, and all of—this...

The slight hint of pallor had touched the other woman's face. But her eyes did not waver. 'Serena was a romantic fool, Luiz,' she responded. 'You will not make me feel guilty for picking up what she so stupidly trampled upon.'

At which point Caroline did actually wince, as her fingers were crushed almost to the bone. Fearing that Luiz was about to do something violent, she burst into speech. 'Introduce me, Luiz,' she prompted lightly.

For a second she thought he was going to ignore her, then he complied, tersely. 'Caroline, this is my mother's sister and my father's widow, Consuela de Vazquez,'

'Hello.' She winged a bright smile across the room towards his stiff-faced aunt. 'I'm so excited about coming here. The castle is so beautiful, isn't it? But I don't think it's as old as it would like to be,' she said, knowing she was babbling like a fluffy blonde idiot, but she didn't care so long as she could overlay the cold hostility threading through the other two. 'It wants to be eleventh century, but I would hazard a guess at only sixteenth century.'

'Seventeenth,' another voice intruded. 'In a fit of pique, when his biggest rival for the hand of a certain lady won the lady's heart because of the size of his home, our ancestor came home here to the valley and built himself his own impressive structure—then married the lady's younger sister. History has a habit of repeating itself in this family—as you will soon learn, I predict.'

Caroline had frozen where she stood, the voice familiar enough to send her floundering in a sea of confusion as a tall, dark, very attractive man appeared from way down at the other end of the long drawing room.

He paused and smiled at her stunned expression, and—completely ignoring Luiz—went on in that same light, self-assured way which had repelled Caroline so much the first time she'd met him.

'Felipe de Vazquez,' he announced himself. 'At your service, Miss Newbury.' It was the man from the lift in Luiz's hotel in Marbella. 'We never did get around to introducing ourselves, did we?' he added with a lazy smile.

'Señor,' she acknowledged. And it was only entrenched good manners that made her accept his outstretched hand.

His fingers closed around hers, cool and smooth and infinitely polite. 'Felipe, please…' he invited. 'We are going to be related very soon, after all…'

Instinctively her other hand tightened in Luiz's and she moved a small fraction closer to him.

It was strange in its own way, but as she found herself making comparisons between Luiz's bone-crushing grip on one of her hands and his half-brother's light clasp, on the other, she knew which grip she felt safer with. But then she was remembering the last time she'd met the man, and the suspicion she'd had then that if she'd tried to break away his grip would have tightened painfully—a sensation that was attacking her again right now.

'Felipe,' she acknowledged politely, and used the moment to slip her hand free and place it flat on Luiz's chest. It was such an obvious declaration of intimacy that no one, not even Luiz, missed that fact. 'Luiz, isn't this a coincidence?' She smiled, keeping her tone light with effort. 'I met your half-brother in the hotel only the other evening, and had no idea he was related to you.'

'Yes,' Luiz drawled. 'What a coincidence.'

It was too soft, too smooth, too lazy to be nice. She knew Luiz, knew the way he worked, the angrier he got the quieter he became.

Did Felipe recognise that? she wondered, when his dark eyes eventually moved to clash with his long lost half-brother's eyes. 'So we meet at last.' Felipe smiled ruefully.

At last? The words hit Caroline like a punch to her solar plexus. Because surely if she had first seen Felipe at the hotel then Luiz must have known he was there?

Obviously not, she concluded, when Luiz replied dryly, 'Not before time, maybe.'

The atmosphere suddenly became very complicated as a confusion of rather unpredictable emotions went skittering around all three of them.

There was ice—a lot of ice. There was curiosity. There was mutual antagonism born from an instant burst of sibling rivalry where both men carefully judged the weight of the other.

She wasn't sure which one of them actually came out on top in that short silent battle, but she certainly knew which one of them held the position of power—no matter what the mental outcome.

'Welcome home, Luiz.' With a slightly wry smile that told her Felipe was acknowledging the same thing, he conceded the higher ground to his half-brother. 'May your next twenty years be more fortuitous than your first twenty...'

It was such an openly cruel thing to say that even his mother released a gasp. So did Caroline, her fingers curling tensely into Luiz's shirt in sheer reflex, as if she was trying to soothe the savage beast before it leapt into action.

But Luiz, to everyone's surprise, laughed. 'Let's certainly hope so,' he agreed. 'Or this place could be in deep trouble—as we all know.'

Tit for tat. Cut and thrust. Luiz had won that round. And he hadn't finished, not by a long shot. 'Which reminds me,' he went on in the brisk cool voice of a true business tycoon, 'I have a lot I need to get through here before our wedding takes place next week. So can we start with a tour of the place, before I settle down to some good old-fashioned household accounting...?'

CHAPTER NINE

CAROLINE was sitting quietly in the window of her allotted valley-facing guestroom when a light tap sounded at her door. For a few precious moments she seriously contemplated not answering.

It had been a horrible few days. Days filled with wariness and tension and eyes watching everything she did and everywhere she went as if they were worried she might decide to run off with the silver!

On top of that, Luiz had taken on the mantle of responsibility here as if it was just another new acquisition in his multinational group. He was quiet, he was calm, he was cool and he was exceedingly businesslike. People—staff, mainly—were already in complete awe of him. They scuttled about like little rabbits earnestly eager to make a good impression. And, all in all, the changes he had put into place already were enough to make the average person gasp.

But this wasn't a business proposition, was it? It was a home—though admittedly a very unusual home. But how did you attempt to point something like that out to a man who barely acknowledged your existence?

Luiz wasn't talking to her. He was angry about something, though she didn't know what. It was difficult to find out when he seemed to have locked himself away inside a suit of armour that wouldn't look out of place in the castle hallway!

She had an itchy feeling his mood stemmed from the fact that she'd met his half-brother before he had. He'd quizzed her about that chance meeting. No—*grilled* her was a better word.

'Where did you meet? How did you meet? What did he say? How did he say it?'

When she'd grown angry and demanded to know why it was so important, he'd simply walked away! Five minutes later she'd seen him standing in the castle grounds with a cellular phone clamped to his ear. Whoever he had been speaking to had been receiving the lash of his angry tongue. Even from up here in this room, looking down into darkness, she had been able to see that.

Since then she had hardly set eyes on him, except to share meals across a dining table with others there to squash any hope of meaningful probing into what was rattling him. They even slept in separate rooms. Now if that was a simple case of maintaining some old-fashioned values here in this time-lock of a valley, then Caroline could understand and accept that. But his cold attitude towards her on every count hurt, even though she kept on telling herself that it shouldn't.

The tap sounded again. On a sigh she got up, and went to answer it. It was one of the little doe eyed maids. 'Excuse me, *señorita*,' she murmured. 'Doña Consuela send me to tell you that the *padre* is here wishing to talk to you?'

The *padre*. Her heart sank. 'All right, thank you, Abril. Will you tell him I'll be down in a few minutes?'

Where was Luiz? she wondered heavily as she crossed to her bathroom. But she knew where Luiz was—or least where he wasn't, she amended. Because Luiz certainly wasn't here in the valley. In fact, Luiz had flown off in the helicopter that had arrived to pick him up early this morning and hadn't been seen or heard of since.

The helicopter landing pad was just one of the changes Luiz had brought into being since they'd arrived here.

He'd had ten men from the village clearing a spot over in the far corner of the garden before Caroline had even got out of bed on that first morning. Another addition he'd had put in at incredible speed was the telecommunications mast erected at the top of the valley—to improve satellite reception, he'd explained over dinner. Apparently you couldn't run a multinational group without good communication.

Shame he didn't apply the same principles to his personal life!

But he didn't, so she now had to go and face the *padre* without knowing a single thing about the wedding proposed for next week, because Luiz hadn't bothered to discuss it with her!

It was going to make her look really good in the *padre*'s eyes if he discovered that he knew more about it than the bride herself!

I'm going to kill you very soon, Luiz Vazquez, she promised him silently as she checked over her cream skirt and lavender top—which were beginning to look a little the worse for wear now, along with the other things she had brought to Spain with her.

When she'd left London she had packed for a three-day short break in a hotel. She had *not* packed for parties in villas and cross-country travelling, or exploring the many admittedly interesting rooms inside a castle!

She found the *padre* waiting for her in the small sitting room the family tended to use during the day because it opened directly into the garden. Tía Consuela was waiting with him, but once she had introduced Caroline to Padre Domingo, she left them alone.

In truth, Caroline felt sorry for Consuela. In the last few months she had lost her husband, seen her own son being disinherited of everything she must know he had every right to consider his, and was about to lose her right to live in the home that had been hers for the last thirty-odd years. Yet the way she had remained on here, taking whatever Luiz wanted to throw at her, had in Caroline's view been rather impressive.

Personally she couldn't have done it. Pride alone would have sent her running for cover well before her estranged nephew could show his face. But, cold and remote though she always was, she had answered all Luiz's intense, sometimes acutely detailed questions about the running of the castle, and was quick to refer him on to those who knew more about the running of the rest of the estate.

While her son did nothing, offered no information and kept himself very much to himself by riding one of his beautiful Andalusian horses out each morning and not coming back until it was so dark that he had to.

Felipe had gone from charmer to brooder in a couple of very short phases. And he might have remained on here, like his mother, but unlike her he did nothing to hide his simmering resentment.

Not that Caroline could really blame him for feeling like that. For, no matter what legal right Luiz had to be here, Felipe, had every excuse for feeling angry and bitterly betrayed by his father.

She just wished she could like him more on a personal level, then maybe she could become a kind of go-between for the two half-brothers, give them a fine line of communication which might help bring them closer together.

'Señorita Newbury,' Padre Domingo greeted her smilingly. 'It is a great pleasure to make your acquaintance at last.'

Taking his proffered hand, Caroline smiled in answer. 'I called to see you yesterday but missed you.'

'I was visiting a *compadre* in the next valley.' He nodded. 'We like to get together once a week to—compare flocks. But I was sorry to be out when you called.'

Pleasantries over, it was a bit difficult to know where to go from there. so she covered her own feeling of awkwardness by inviting him to sit down. 'Can I get you a drink?' she offered. 'Tea, coffee—or something cooler, perhaps?'

But he shook his white head and with a slight wave of one beautifully slender hand invited her to sit before he would allow himself to do so.

'You liked our little church?' he enquired when they had both settled into Louis the Fifteenth chairs still wearing their original upholstery.

Caroline smiled. 'It's the prettiest church I've ever set foot in,' she answered honestly. 'But then this whole valley is the prettiest I've ever stepped foot in,' she added with a warm twinkle in her eyes.

'But very isolated,' the father pointed out.

'Part of its charm,' Caroline immediately defended, with that same teasing twinkle.

'And also very—Catholic...'

Ah, she thought, losing the twinkle. 'Is that going to be a problem?' she asked. 'Luiz and I marrying in your church with me not being a Roman Catholic, I mean?' she went on, thinking silently—where are you Luiz? You should have seen this problem arising!

In his neat black robe with its round white collar the father eyed her thoughtfully from his thin, wise face. 'Is it a problem for you?' he countered eventually.

'Only if you expect me to make a sudden conversion,' she answered candidly.

'No.' He shook his head. 'I do not expect that sacrifice of you—as I would hope your English church would not expect the same thing of Luiz if the situation were reversed. See, we are emancipated here.' He smiled then. 'Even in our sleepy little valley.'

'But there is a problem?' Caroline prompted shrewdly. It was written in his thoughtful stare.

'The problem is more one of—sincerity than religion,' he murmured slowly, and when Caroline began to frown in confusion he seemed to come to a decision. 'Let me be blunt, Miss Newbury,' he said. 'It has come to my attention that you and Don Luiz are intending to exchange sacred vows with each other which may not be exactly truthful, and indeed are merely a means to a rather sinister end...'

Sinister? Caroline picked up on the word and pondered it frowningly, suddenly very wary as to where the priest was going with this. 'Are you trying to suggest that every marriage in your church has been a perfect love-match?' she questioned, aware that if any culture was known for arranging loveless marriages, then surely Spain had to be it!

'In this particular case, it is only your marriage to Don Luiz that I am concerned with,' the priest replied smoothly. 'You met for the first time only five days ago, I have been led to believe. Within hours of that meeting Don Luiz was announcing your intention to marry and your own father was collapsing due to the shock. It has also been suggested that your father is in debt to Don Luiz for a rather large amount of money which may well be the motive behind this—arrangement.'

'Suggested by whom?' Even as the full weight of his words came as a bit of a blow Caroline's hackles were rising—and it showed in the sudden glint in her amethyst eyes.

'The source of my information is not really important,' he dismissed with a wave of one slender hand. 'My concern here is really for you, *señorita*,' he explained. 'I came here today with serious concerns that you were being—coerced into the marriage for reasons beyond your control.'

'Are you trying to tell me, that you are refusing to marry Luiz and I?' she challenged, coming stiffly to her feet. She simply had not been expecting him to question their sincerity like this.

Inherent good manners made him rise to his feet also. 'No,' he denied. 'Don Luiz is the new *conde* here in this valley. If he tells me to marry him to a lady gagged and chained to his side, then I marry them.' He shrugged, adding with a wry smile, 'There, the old ways are not quite dead, heh?' And now it was his turn to flick her a twinkling smile.

But Caroline was in no mood to twinkle back at him. 'Then let me put your mind at rest,' she said coolly. 'Your information is wrong,' she declared. 'Luiz and I have known each other for seven years. We have been *lovers* for seven years.' Which was not quite a lie, even if it wasn't quite the truth. But in this situation it served her purpose very nicely to make that point.

Surprised though the priest undoubtedly was by her correction, it didn't faze him. 'But have you *loved* Don Luiz for seven years?' he threw right back.

Love? Caroline repeated to herself, and smiled a half-smile that was more rueful than cynical, though she had a feeling it should have been the other way round. 'I've *always* loved Luiz,' she responded dryly. 'But if you are going to ask me if he feels the same way about me,' she added, 'then please don't.'

'Then of course I will not,' he instantly conceded, and with eyes which conveyed a gentle apology for making her feel compelled to add that final remark, he gently touched one of Caroline's hands. 'Forgive my intrusion into what you clearly feel is your private business. But I had to be sure that you cared for Don Luiz before I could carry out his father's last wish.'

His father's last wish? Her eyes grew curious, but the

priest had already turned away and was walking across the room to where a rather bulky attaché case she hadn't noticed before lay on a table by the door.

'I am now going to place something into your care *señorita*,' he explained, 'that I must make you promise to guard with your life and show to no one…'

For some obscure reason, watching him open the attaché case as he spoke those words made her feel suddenly afraid. 'If it's something that will hurt Luiz, then you can keep it,' she told him.

'I commend your desire to protect him,' he replied, turning with what looked like several thin ledgers in his hands. 'And—yes—these will hurt Don Luiz if he ever sees them. He is, of course, the one exception to the promise I am about to make you swear. Can you read Spanish as well as you speak it?' he asked suddenly.

Caroline nodded. She had spent most of her summers since she was a small child right here in Spain, and that meant that Spanish had become her second language.

'Then, having read these—' he indicated the ledgers '—I will leave it to your discretion to decide whether you think he needs to know all that has been written in here…'

He began to approach her, and it was all Caroline could do not to snatch her trembling hands behind her back. For whatever it was he was about to give her, she knew she didn't want. He saw it in her face and paused two steps away.

'These are the diaries of Don Luiz's *papá*,' he informed her. 'Left in my care long before Don Carlos was taken ill. They explain why Don Luiz inherits all and Don Felipe very little. They explain why Don Luiz has been his *papá*'s beneficiary for the whole of his thirty-five years. So take them,' he urged. 'Read them and understand—for Luiz's sake, please, *señorita*…'

Sombrely he held them out to her. Reluctantly Caroline

accepted them, her fingers turning cold as they closed around the diaries; worse her heart felt as if it had turned to stone. She didn't know why, didn't understand what any of this was about. But she knew one thing as surely as she knew her name was Caroline: these books were dark things—dark and awful things.

'I'll read them,' she promised.

The priest nodded in silent understanding of the expression on her face and simply turned without another word to take his leave. But as he reached the door he paused, glanced back at her, still standing where he had left her in the middle of the room with the books clutched between tense white fingers.

'You know, *señorita,*' he murmured thoughtfully, 'it is, I think, quite a curious coincidence that you should have known Don Luiz for seven years. For it was also seven years ago that he first agreed to come here and meet his *papá* for the first time, only to abruptly change his mind. The reason he gave for that change, was that he had met the woman he was going to marry. Courting her, it seemed, was more important to him then than meeting his father. He did, though, promise to wed her here, in the church of the Valle de los Angeles, as was tradition. It seems he is about to keep that promise, hmm?'

He smiled. Then, before she could remark on that fresh piece of shock information, he was turning away again. 'Read the diaries, Miss Newbury. And learn about the man who loves you as much I think as you love him,' he advised as he left her alone.

Hours later she wished to God that she hadn't read the diaries. She wished to God that the whole Vazquez family had kept to their old ways and stayed right out of Luiz's life.

She hid the books away in her room on the top of a great oak wardrobe that stood against a wall. Then she went outside into the afternoon heat and paced the garden, lost in dark thoughts filled with heartache and betrayal and the cruel sacrifice of one innocent child for the sake of another.

'History repeating itself,' Felipe had called it. Luiz had called it feuds and fortunes. Caroline called it unforgivable. And if Luiz knew only half of what she had just discovered via those diaries, then it was no wonder he had shut himself away inside an invisible suit of armour since coming here. This family was poison to anyone who touched them. Which brought to mind yet another remark made by his uncle the doctor. 'Take a food-taster with you,' he'd advised. He too knew that there was poison in this beautiful place.

The only bit of good she had gleaned from those diaries had been confirmation that the priest had been telling the truth about Luiz's intentions towards her seven years ago. But even that truth had its poisonous side.

For, if Luiz had loved her then, why had he gone from her arms directly to a card table to try and bankrupt her father night after night?

When the sound of a helicopter came whirring over the mountain, she wished Luiz had stayed away. She was still too upset, too confused. She needed more time to think, to absorb, and decide how much she was going to tell him about what she had learned today—if she was going to tell him anything at all.

Yet as the helicopter landed on its newly prepared site she found herself standing there waiting for him. As he stepped down onto solid ground her heart began to fill with a multitude of emotions she just couldn't separate.

Dressed in a dark grey business suit with needle-sharp tailoring, bright white shirt and a steel-grey tie, he looked the true tycoon, the true nobleman. In fact no one looking at his lean, dark, proudly arrogant profile would believe he had spent the first twenty years of his life living literally from hand to mouth.

He also looked sombre, she noticed, as if the worries of the whole world had suddenly descended upon him. She knew the feeling, since she was experiencing the very same thing herself.

The fault of this valley? Was the fatal flaw in its beauty its need to taint all that came here?

Fanciful though she knew she was being, she knew suddenly that she needed to be close to him—very badly. She also knew that she needed to get away from here, if only for a little while, to think, to regain some perspective.

So the moment he was free of the helicopter's lethal blades she began walking across the lawn to meet him. He saw her coming towards him and stopped and stared, as if he was seeing his life's dream, before those heavily defended eyes were hiding as usual.

And for no other reason than because she needed to, she wound her arms around his neck and kissed him urgently. His surprise was evident in the moment of tension she felt grip him, and for a couple of horrible seconds she thought he was actually going to thrust her away.

Then his arms looped around her—tightly enough to crush her against his hard-packed body—and he began to kiss her back with a hunger that easily matched her own.

It was like finding herself after being lost in a dark place for days upon end. Whatever else was between them that didn't make sense, this always—always—felt so very right.

He broke the kiss. She would have been content to remain right there, kissing him like this for ever. But those dark eyes of his were frowning down at her, probing the whitened pallor even the kiss had not managed to dispel. 'What's wrong?' he demanded. 'Who has upset you?'

Caroline just shook her head. 'I missed you, that's all,'

she told him huskily. 'I've been missing you for day:
though you didn't seem to notice.'

'I noticed,' he murmured gruffly. 'I just thought it wa
better if I gave you time to yourself to—come to term
with all of this…'

'All of this' being the fairytale castle standing behin
them, that had suddenly become a very haunted castle fo
Caroline.

'I don't need time to come to terms with it,' she denie
'I have something similar of my own in England, if yo
recall—though I admit it isn't as grand as this. But–
Luiz…' Despite trying to, she couldn't keep the strain fror
creeping into her tone. 'Can we get away from here for
little while?' she begged. 'Just you and me, somewhere–
ordinary? Can that thing fly us out—just for a couple d
hours? Please?'

'You don't like it here,' he sighed.

'I love it here,' she insisted, knowing it was a lie an
that at that precise moment she hated this valley and ev
erything in it. 'I just need some time away from it for
little while. Is that too much to ask?'

'No.' He was still frowning, because he knew she wasn
telling him the entire truth, but one of his hands flicked
staying motion at the pilot aimed to make him keep th
engine running. 'Where would you like to go? T
Marbella?' he suggested. 'We can be there in—'

But Caroline was shaking her head. 'There's this litt
place I know. A secret place,' she whispered confidingl
and her eyes began to warm with sensual promise. 'It ha
the softest bed on this earth, I think. No air conditionir
and a bathroom down the hall. But it has the most wor
derfully cool and crinkly starched cotton sheets on the be
and there won't be a frosty face in sight…'

He was gazing down at her as if having to convinc
himself that she was suggesting what it seemed that sh

was. And Caroline's breath snagged in her chest while she waited for some kind of response.

Agreement or rejection? He was so unpredictable, burning hot, turning cold. Pounce and retreat. Trying to pre-empt his response was impossible, she acknowledged as his silence began to sew fine threads of tension beneath the surface of her skin.

Then a sleek brow arched, mockery spiked his eyes. 'Is this your ladylike way of inviting me for a dirty weekend, by any chance?' he questioned sardonically.

Put like that, it sounded so brazen that she felt her cheeks go red—then she caught the beginnings of his lazy smile and she smiled too. 'I suppose I am,' she admitted. 'Though if you prefer the company of your family,' she added innocently, 'then I am open to compromise...'

His dark head went back and he started laughing. It was the best sound she had heard in days. Her heart literally swelled on the pleasure of it, and he was still laughing after he'd captured her hand and walked her back towards the waiting helicopter.

Neither saw his half-brother watching them from the shrubbery. Neither saw the malignant glint in his eyes as he watched them lift off and fly away.

They were dropped off in a clearing just outside Los Aminos and walked into the village hand in hand. They must look an odd kind of couple, Caroline decided wryly, with Luiz in his razor-sharp suit and her in her simple cream skirt and lavender top.

The hotel proprietor was the same, and his eyes rounded as they stepped through the door. At the appearance of an exorbitant amount of money, the round-eyed look changed to one of obsequious respect which produced the same key to the same room with exactly the same bed.

'I'm even wearing the same clothes,' Caroline whispered to Luiz as they climbed the stairs hand in hand.

'And the same pink bloom on your cheeks,' he added teasingly. And as the bloom deepened on her first realisation of what she had actually dared to propose here, he shut the door with one hand and reached for her with the other.

They didn't go back to the castle that night. It was a wonderful warm, enchanted experience, where Caroline felt as if she had found the lover she had carelessly lost— not once but twice, when she thought about the last few lonely days.

They made love as if there would be no tomorrow. They touched and kissed and caressed each other as if this would be their last opportunity. It was all very hot, very serious and intense.

'You were my first true love,' she softly confessed to him at one point.

His eyes turned black in their sleepy sockets. 'And you, believe it or not, were mine,' he replied.

But—no, she couldn't accept that. For a man who loved someone didn't take her family for every penny he could squeeze out of it, she thought sadly, and to bury the sadness she took his dark face between her hands and brought his mouth crushing down on top of her own.

Maybe he sensed her sadness, maybe he saw it just before she buried it away. Whatever—something thrust him onto a whole new plane of passion. It was devastatingly rich, and left her floating in a place of boneless satiation from which she didn't return for ages.

When she eventually did decide to open her eyes, she found herself curled into Luiz's side with her cheek resting on his shoulder; it was growing dark outside.

'We didn't tell anyone we were leaving,' she remarked—without much concern for the omission.

'I sent the pilot back to make our excuses,' he replied. 'They are to expect us when they see us.'

He sounded so arrogant then, so much the lord of his valley that she released a soft chuckle. The sound brought his hand to her nape so he could make her look at him.

'That was the first sound of genuine amusement I've heard from you since we met again,' he told her huskily.

'What did you expect?' She pouted. 'When you've done nothing but blackmail and bully me!'

It was supposed to be a tease, but Luiz didn't smile. Instead his eyes remained darkly probing. 'I didn't bully you to get you here tonight,' he quietly pointed out.

'No,' she agreed. She had been the one doing the bullying this time.

'Are you ready to explain to me now what happened today to make you want to run away like this?'

So he knew she hadn't been telling the truth back at the castle. She turned her face down again, and began watching the way her fingers were drawing whirls into his chest hair.

'I had a visitor,' she said, deciding to come clean with the truth—or part of the truth anyway. 'The village priest,' she explained.

Luiz had gone still; even his heart seemed to have slowed beneath her resting cheek. 'And…?' he prompted very quietly.

'And he wanted to know if our planned wedding was a sham.' She smiled.

'Was he threatening not to marry us?'

Clever, quick Luiz, she thought. 'No,' she denied. 'In fact he assured me that if *el conde* came to his altar with his bride chained and gagged he would marry them.'

'Then what was his point?'

Now there was a question, she thought, and on a soft rueful laugh she sat up, to run her fingers through her tangled hair. 'His point was, I think,' she began slowly, choosing her words with care, 'to make me aware that

certain—rumours were circulating the valley about the sin
cerity of our feelings for one another.'

'Rumours?' he repeated.

'Mmm.' She nodded. 'Apparently it is being said tha
you and I met for the first time only a few days befor
you brought me here as your bride...'

'And you said—what?'

He hadn't moved a single muscle since this had started
and Caroline now had her back towards him, so sh
couldn't see his face. The worst thing about Luiz, she tol
herself grimly, was his annoying ability to speak withou
giving a single hint as to what he was thinking.

'I told him the information was inaccurate,' she said
'That we had known each other for seven years. Then
lied a bit,' she added with a shrug, 'and told him we ha
been lovers for seven years...'

Only it hadn't felt much like a lie when she had said it
she recalled. In fact it was probably closer to the truth tha
anyone would believe—in her case at least.

'To which he said what?'

'You're very good at this,' she remarked, turning he
head to level him with a dry look.

Two sleek black brows rose in enquiry. Her stomac
muscles leapt. He's such a sexy devil, she thought help
lessly.

'The Spanish Inquisition,' she explained. 'In fact yo
remind me of a dripping tap. You just steadily and relent
lessly drop your questions until you get to know what i
is you're after.'

'To which he said—what?' he repeated, and ther
wasn't a single alteration in those black holes for eyes.

She looked away again, and a heavy sigh whispere
from her because the truth was out of bounds. And ther
was another problem she had been worrying over since th
priest's visit.

'I think he was trying to warn us that someone is making trouble for you,' she said. 'Someone is feeding rumours about the valley that you and I are a sham—which is, I presume, their way of making sure we will never gain the people's respect. The other rumour is that you have more or less bought me from my father. Now, who but you and I know anything about that?'

'You think I have been telling tales?'

It was such a ridiculous suggestion that she laughed. 'You mean it *is* possible to get blood from a stone?' she mocked—then released another sigh. 'What's worrying me, Luiz,' she explained, 'is that someone has to have been spying on us. And it sends creepy feelings down my spine just to think of it.' She even shuddered.

A hand came to her naked back and soothed the shudders. 'The spy in this case we already know, *querida,*' he informed her quietly. 'And because we also know he has some right to be bitter enough about the situation to spread rumours which may place us in a poor light, we will allow him a small—indiscretion. It is, after all, all he believes he has left to survive on right now...'

He was talking about Felipe. The name didn't need saying. 'Okay,' she agreed, and curled herself back around him, needing to say more but afraid to say more in case too much came pouring out.

'Okay?' he repeated quizzically. 'Just like that?'

'Mmm.' She snuggled herself into his warm, muscled strength. 'This is too nice to spoil by talking about nasty things. And anyway, I've got far more pressing concerns on my mind right now.'

His eyes began to gleam, the humour she could see running through them heating her blood.

'Shopping!' she announced in mock censure. 'I'm talking about my need to go shopping for some fresh clothes, since you abducted me with only enough clothes to last me three days! *And* I want to buy a really expensive bridal dress with all the trimmings,' she tagged on, right out of the blue. 'Because if I *have* to marry you then I insist that you let me do it in style!'

In the startled silence that followed his eyes narrowed slightly, as if he was reading a return to the old bitterness in what she'd said.

It wasn't there. And a moment later she was being loved again—which she much preferred to talking.

They stayed in that hot, dark, old-fashioned hotel room all night, and made love and ate paella cooked specially by the hotel proprietor's very eager wife, and slept in each other's arms and awoke there. It was the first time Caroline had woken up to find him still there beside her. It made an oddly painful impression on her to realise that.

The next day Luiz had them flown to Cordoba, where Caroline played the future bride to a wealthy man to the hilt and shopped until she dropped. She was bright, she was flirtatious, and she was enchanting to be with. And if Luiz looked at her strangely now and then, as if he was trying to work out what was making her behave this way, Caroline just smiled at him, or kissed him, or demanded more money from him, diverting the risk of any questions.

Because how did you explain to someone like him that while reading his father's diaries she had come face to face with the real Luiz Vazquez? She understood him now, and hurt for him, and loved him more deeply than she dared let herself dwell upon.

Even if Luiz could never come to love her in the same way that she loved him, then she could live with that— just. Because the other thing she had learned while reading those diaries was that love was not automatically given back by right.

CHAPTER TEN

THEY arrived back at the valley to find yet another wave of changes had been wrought while they had been away. The garden had been decorated with fairylights, the castle itself cleaned and polished to within an inch of its life, and the construction of a long banqueting table was in the process of being completed in the main hall as they walked in the door.

'You are pulling out all the stops, I see.' Felipe's lazy drawl emerged before he did, from a dark corner of the hall.

He had a habit of doing that, Caroline thought as she took a small step closer to Luiz. His hand closed round her hand.

'If one has to marry then let no detail be overlooked,' he mocked. 'No festive trick be ignored.'

His derision was acute. Caroline wanted to hit him for being so mean-mouthed. But Luiz took the criticism in his stride. 'It must be the hotelier in me.' He smiled. 'If there is one thing I have learned to do well, then it is to put on a good party.'

'With the relatives obediently gathered around you to help you celebrate.' Felipe nodded. 'It is quite extraordinary what healthy quarterly allowances can make people do that they normally would not deign to tolerate.'

'Is that why you decided to hang around, Felipe?' Luiz countered curiously. 'Because you see the need to secure your quarterly allowance?'

'I have money of my own,' he declared, but Luiz had

hit a raw nerve. 'My father did not leave me quite destitute.'

'No, he left you a *finca* in the Sierra Nevada and the means to make a success of it, if you could be bothered to try.'

'While you get all of—this…' Felipe's smile was rancid. 'Tell me…' Suddenly he turned his attention on Caroline. She stiffened instantly, sensing it was her turn to receive the whip of his nasty tongue. 'How did the poker game between your father and Luiz end? There are a lot of people who must be dying to know…'

He must have been there, in the casino, when Luiz had issued the challenge to her father, Caroline realised as she felt her cheeks grow pale. Her hand twitched in Luiz's, in a silent plea for him to answer that question.

He tightened his grip a little, but surprised her by saying absolutely nothing. Instead he lifted his free hand and gave a sharp click of his fingers. Without warning, Vito Martinez materialised in front of them. Big and broad and built to smash rocks against, he stood waiting for Luiz to speak.

'Escort Caroline to her room, Vito,' he instructed, without removing his gaze from Felipe. 'And remain there until I come…'

Caroline's skin was prickling, and the shivery sense that he was issuing some kind of dire warning to Felipe with his security guard's daunting presence was enough to keep her silent when Luiz let go of her hand and instructed quietly, 'Go with Vito. Felipe and I have a few—things we need to discuss in private…'

She went, but she felt sick. She didn't look back, but she could almost feel the two men sizing each other up as if for battle. 'What's going to happen?' she whispered to Vito.

'They will talk,' he answered simply. 'As Luiz said.'

'I don't like him,' she confessed, finding herself moving that little bit closer to this big tower of a man Luiz had made her escort.

'Few people do,' Vito replied. That was all, but it seemed to say more than enough. Both Luiz and Vito had Felipe's measure. And that meant that if Felipe had been checking up on them then Luiz had certainly been checking up on him—using this man she was walking beside to do the checking, she suspected.

Vito didn't leave her even when she slipped away to use her bathroom; he was still standing by the door when she got back.

'You've known Luiz a long time, haven't you?' she questioned curiously.

'Since we were both nine years old,' Vito replied.

Which placed them, by her reckoning, in an orphanage together. 'So you are friends,' she concluded, smiling wryly to herself because she was remembering her own thoughts from the other day, when she'd been sitting in the back of Luiz's car while Vito drove her.

'He saved my life once,' Vito answered, but didn't elaborate, even though Caroline stared at him in disbelief because she couldn't imagine anyone having to save this man's life for him. He was just too big, too *everything* surely, to be put into that kind of danger.

The purchases she'd made while they'd been away began to arrive then, diverting her attention. And a few more minutes after that Luiz arrived. With a quiet word in Vito's ear he dismissed the other man, who left with a grim nod of his head that made Caroline shiver.

'Why the need of a bodyguard?' she demanded, the moment they were alone again. 'Am I in some kind of danger I should know about?'

'No,' Luiz denied. 'Not while I'm still breathing at any rate.'

'So *you're* the one who's in danger,' she therefore concluded.

'Nobody is in danger!' he denied.

'Then why the bodyguard?' she repeated stubbornly.

'Escort,' he corrected. 'He was sent to escort you up here simply to make a point, okay? '

No, it wasn't okay. And her face told Luiz that. 'All right,' he sighed out heavily. 'Felipe would like to stop the wedding from taking place,' he said. 'That much is patently obvious. But how far he would go to stop it I am not entirely sure. So I am protecting my weak spots.'

'And I am a weak spot.'

Suddenly his laziest grin appeared. 'Oh, a very weak spot,' he murmured seductively, and began to pace suggestively towards her.

'Don't you dare!' she protested, putting out a hand to ward him off. 'Not here in this house! Not until we are married!' she added, chin up, amethyst eyes challenging. 'I *will* have your respect *el conde!*' she insisted when he took another step towards her.

He stopped. She had to fight to keep her disappointment from showing. Luiz grinned again, because he saw it anyway. 'If I touched you now, you would go up in smoke,' he challenged softly.

'If you touched me now, I probably would,' she ruefully agreed.

'Then I won't,' he assured her.

'Oh,' she said, and didn't even try to hide her disappointment this time.

'Protocol,' he explained. 'Thanks for reminding me that in this house I must respect all bridal traditions.'

If Caroline was aware that she had changed a lot in the last twenty-four hours, then she was also aware that Luiz had changed too. Gone was a lot of the stiff tension he had brought with them into the valley, and what she saw now was a wonderfully charming, lazily relaxed and very sensually motivated man—in private anyway.

It was that recognition that sent her walking into his arms. 'Just one chaste kiss, then,' she offered invitingly, and snaked even closer to him when his arms slid caressingly about her.

'Chaste?' he mocked.

'Mmm,' she said. But there was nothing chaste in the way they stood there amongst a sea of unopened packages for long, very unsatisfying minutes.

'I have to go,' Luiz groaned out reluctantly.

Go? 'Go where?' she demanded.

'Work,' he said, glancing at his watch. And suddenly he was the frustratingly brisk and businesslike Luiz. 'I have things to do before our wedding. And I need to get out of the valley before it grows too dark to fly...'

'But we've only just arrived!'

'Don't blame me!' he countered at her look of dismay. 'You're the one who has put my schedule back twenty-four hours! A deliciously welcome twenty-four hours, I will admit,' he added ruefully. 'But now I have to play catch-up. So you won't see me again until we meet at the church.'

'Luiz!' she cried out as he walked off to the door. 'W-what about your weak spot?' she reminded him anxiously.

'Vito is staying.' It seemed to say it all. 'Anything you want or are worried about, you go to him.'

'Because he owes you his life and therefore will do anything for you?'

That stopped him. He turned to stare at her in surprise. 'You managed to get him to tell you that?' He sounded truly shocked. 'Well, that's a first,' he drawled.

'What did you do?' she asked. 'Haul him out of the razor fight that put all those marks on his face?'

'No,' he denied, and suddenly he wasn't smiling. 'I

hauled him out of prison and gave him a life. And that wasn't kind, Caroline,' he told her grimly.

He was right; it wasn't. 'I'm sorry,' she mumbled contritely.

He nodded. 'See you Wednesday.'

He was going to go, and she didn't want him to go with bad words between them. 'I like him, actually,' she confessed. 'Mainly because he's so loyal to you, I think. You didn't know Felipe was even staying at your hotel, did you?' she then asked, on a complete change of subject.

'He booked in under a different name,' Luiz explained.

'And proceeded to shadow both me and my father,' she mused frowningly. 'He knew who I was—knew who my father was. Which tells you you have a mole in your midst somewhere, Luiz.'

He nodded. 'I'm aware of that—and dealing with it.'

'Does all of this make my father another weak spot?' she asked.

For some reason the question had him turning to study her curiously. 'Yes,' he replied quietly.

She released a sigh and began to look fretful again. 'Are you protecting him too?'

'Undoubtedly,' he assured her, in a strange tone that matched the strange expression he was wearing on his face. 'He will be here, safe and sound, to give your hand to me on our wedding day. Have no fear about that, *querida*.'

Then he was gone, leaving Caroline to stand there staring at the last spot he had been standing on, wondering why she was feeling so very chilled again when surely what he had just said should have been reassuring?

A tap at the door broke her free from whatever it was that was holding her, and she opened it to find Abril, the little maid standing there. 'Don Luiz send me to help you unpack your purchases,' she explained.

Caroline was glad of the diversion. It seemed nothing here in this valley could stay happy for long. Together she and Abril unpacked box after box bearing the names of designers Caroline would never have normally been able to afford to buy.

When it came to the dress she had chosen to marry Luiz in, the two of them unpacked it together, with a kind of hushed air of expectancy that increased to a breathless delight when the dress was finally hanging on its satin-covered hanger from the tall wardrobe door.

'This is beautiful, *señorita*,' Abril sighed out wistfully.

Yes, it was, Caroline agreed, smiling softly to herself when she remembered the way she had sent Luiz off to get himself some coffee somewhere while she'd chosen the dress on her own. He'd been all lazy mockery as he strode away. But she suspected that secretly he'd rather liked the idea of her choosing a dress aimed exclusively to please him.

'You have a sweetheart of your own?' Caroline asked curiously.

The young maid blushed. 'No,' she denied. 'But when I do, I would wish to marry him in something as lovely as this...'

She was lightly fingering the delicate lace when the idea came to Caroline. She hadn't given a thought to it before, but it suddenly struck her now, when it was almost too late to do anything about it, that she was going to have no friends of her own here to help her dress, or share her excitement, or even one to stand as her witness.

Luiz Vazquez, the fine-detail man, seemed to have overlooked that small but important point.

'Abril...' she murmured slowly, forming the request even as she spoke it out loud. 'Would you do something very—special for me?'

'Of course, *señorita*,' the maid instantly replied.

'If I can get a dress here in time—a pretty dress for you to wear—would you be my bridesmaid?'

For a terrible moment she thought she'd actually horrified the poor girl, she was so still and silent. Then, 'Oh *señorita*,' she breathed. 'Do you really mean it?'

The doe eyes were suddenly shining with pleasure. 'Yes I mean it.' Caroline found herself smiling too. 'You must have noticed that I am here on my own,' she pointed out sagely. 'My family and friends are all in England, and though my father is coming I will have no one else. It would be nice, don't you think, to have someone from the valley to stand beside me?'

'It would be an honour,' the young girl answered gravely. 'But, I will have to ask permission of Doña Consuela before I may say absolutely that I will do this,' she added anxiously.

'Of course,' Caroline said instantly, not bothering to point out that it was really Luiz's permission the maid should be seeking. And since she knew what his answer would be without having to ask him, Caroline didn't think that was a problem.

'I'll ask her,' she decided. Abril looked relieved. 'In fact I'll go and do it now, while you finish up here, okay?'

Nothing like striking while the iron is hot, she told herself bracingly as she went in search of Luiz's aunt. But she was beginning to half wish she hadn't started this, being a coward deep down inside.

She found Doña Consuela in the main drawing room. She was just standing there, staring out of the window, watching the construction taking place on the lawn outside. And there was a sad, lonely, isolated look to her stance that touched Caroline's heart a little, even though she now knew exactly how effective this woman had been in ruining Luiz's *mamá*'s life.

'Consuela...' she prompted.

She hadn't even heard Caroline come in the room, she was so lost inside her own bleak thoughts. But she turned at the sound of her name, her expression as smoothly composed as it always was.

Sometimes her relationship to Luiz is all too clear, Caroline mused ruefully.

'I wondered if you would mind if I asked your advice about something,' she ventured carefully—though why she had changed from making it a polite request to the more gentle quest for advice she was not entirely sure—unless it was because Consuela had looked a little like Luiz then.

Luiz when he was hiding hurt, she extended sadly.

'Of course,' the older woman agreed. 'If you think my advice will be of use.'

Taking a deep breath, Caroline explained what she wanted to do and why she wanted to do it. Consuela listened to her without expression, and it was therefore a surprise when the other woman smiled a brief, rather bleak smile and said, 'You are a nice person, *señorita*. It will be comforting to know that I will be leaving the valley in the charge of someone so sensitive.'

'Luiz cares too, you know,' Caroline declared, instantly on the defensive, because she hadn't expected approval from this particular source and was therefore searching for hidden criticism.

The Condesa's smile grew wry. 'I know that,' she said. 'And, yes, it would be a perfect touch for you to have Abril as your maid of honour. The people of the valley will love you for doing it. Give the child my blessing and tell her she is relieved of all her normal duties so she can devote her time to her new exciting role.'

While you do what? Caroline wanted to ask. Keep fading ever more into the shadows of this place that has been your home for so many years?

'What will you do?' she asked impulsively. 'When yo
leave here?'

The smile was wry again. 'So, Luiz intends to have m
banished,' the other woman said. 'I did wonder.'

Caroline felt absolutely horrified that she had inadve
tently stepped into something she should not. 'I don
know,' she answered awkwardly. 'Luiz doesn't discuss h
family with me.'

'No, I don't suppose he does,' the Condesa murmure
and turned back to the window. It was a dismissal in an
one's books. Feeling like some kind of heel, Caroline too
herself out of the room without daring to utter anoth
word.

Next she went to search out Vito. She found him in th
garden, overlooking the setting out of what looked as if
was going to be a wooden dance floor beneath a red an
white striped awning.

'Vito—' She touched his arm to gain his attention the
instantly withdrew her fingers again when they tingled a
if they'd just touched solid rock. 'Do you think Luiz wou
mind if I put his helicopter to use?' she said.

He swung around so lightly for a man of his size th
Caroline was startled. 'Why?' he demanded sharply. 'Wh
do you want the helicopter for? What's wrong?'

'Nothing,' she assured him, but even as she spoke h
eyes were flicking in all directions, and he seemed to gro
another few inches, like a bear getting ready to enfold i
prey. Or, in her case, to protect its cub, she amended ru
fully.

'I need the helicopter to run an errand for me,' she sai
'A special errand.' Then she went on to explain...

She was just finishing some breakfast on the morning
her wedding day when her father arrived in Luiz's hel
copter. The moment she saw it was him climbing out sl

was up and running, out of the hall and out into the sunshine, to meet him halfway across the lawn.

'Oh, Daddy,' she sobbed, and launched herself at him. 'How could you just walk away from me like that?'

'Don't fuss, Caro. I'm fine!' he censured irritably as she began a detailed check for any physical signs of poor health.

'You don't look fine,' she told him, seeing the changes in him even if he didn't think they were there. He looked older and thinner and— She sighed unhappily.

'Some place—this,' he ventured, deliberately changing the subject, Caroline suspected. 'Never seen anything quite like it. Coming in over the top of that mountain actually took my breath away. Did you know seven years ago that Luiz was heir to all of this?'

'No.' She was trying to catch his eye, but he wouldn't let her, and his hands were grimly keeping her at arm's length. 'It wouldn't have made any difference to the way I felt about him if I had,' she added absently. 'Will you please look at me?' she said impatiently.

He flicked his eyes to hers. She saw the guilt, the shame and the misery, and her own eyes filled with tears. 'I love you so much,' she choked. 'And I've been worried about you!'

His defences collapsed. On a ragged sigh he tugged her to him and wrapped his arms around her tight. 'And him?' he questioned gruffly. 'Do you love him?'

'Like a second skin,' she replied. 'But then I always have done, you already knew that.'

'Yes, I always knew it,' he confirmed heavily. 'But I'm still sorry for getting you into this dreadful mess.'

'No mess,' she denied, then repeated it when she saw his disbelieving look. 'No mess, Daddy. Luiz is what I want. He's what I've always wanted.'

He grimaced. 'But not handed to him on a plate like a damned sacrifice.'

'I'm no sacrifice either!' she informed him crossly. 'Or are you trying to imply that Luiz feels nothing for me in return? Because if you are,' she continued angrily, 'then maybe you should just turn around and go away again.'

'I'm not implying anything.' He sighed again. 'Good grief,' he added. 'The man has twice gone to big enough lengths in his attempts to get you to this day…'

Twice? Caroline felt that chill hit her spine again. 'What do you mean twice?' she demanded.

'Nothing,' he grunted, going all shifty-eyed. 'Well, would you look at that?' he then exclaimed in surprise, diverting her attention to the spot he was looking at near the castle entrance. 'What's he doing here? He never told me he knew Luiz!'

He never told me… Caroline repeated to herself as she too turned to stare at Felipe. And so many, many things began to slide into place. Her own father was Luiz's mole, though unwittingly.

Oh, Daddy, she thought sighingly. And when he went to go and speak to Felipe she stopped him. 'Watch him, Pops,' she warned, and just the quiet use of her childhood name for him was enough to alert Sir Edward to trouble. 'Watch every single word you say to him and watch your back.'

'Why?' he frowned. 'Who is he?'

'He's Luiz's half-brother—the man who thinks he should have inherited all of this…'

Enlightenment came to him as quickly as it had come to his daughter. His soft curse confirmed it.

The helicopter lifted off then, rendering words useless as the sounds of its rotors filled the air. Her father seemed to use the time the helicopter took to sweep off down the valley to come to some kind of decision.

'Let's go somewhere where we can talk in private,' he said flatly. 'I have something I want to say to you...'

Caroline wanted to talk to Luiz. She *needed* to talk to Luiz. But the juggernaut called her wedding was now rolling ahead at full speed, and Luiz, she assumed, was already waiting for her at the tiny church in the centre of the village where, since her father had arrived, so had gathered the full Vazquez family, to witness the event taking place.

'You look beautiful, *señorita,*' Abril's gentle voice brought Caroline's anxious eyes into focus on the mirror she was standing in front of.

The ankle-length ivory crêpe gown was quite simply sensational, even if she did think so herself. The corset-like bodice skimmed her slender ribcage and scooped low over the creamy slopes of her breasts, and the little off-the-shoulder sleeves added just the right touch of vulnerable charm to a bride who was about to walk down a church aisle towards her bridegroom.

To add a final touch, her full-length veil was secured to her head by a delicate diamond tiara. The overall effect was simplicity itself—her style, her way of doing things.

Her wedding.

Luiz, she told her amethyst eyes via the mirror. You are about to marry Luiz.

But how could Luiz want to marry her, knowing how badly she misjudged him seven years ago?

Luiz never said he *wanted* to marry you, only that he *needed* to marry someone, she reminded those anxious amethyst eyes. And all you've been doing these last few days is pretending that this is a marriage made in heaven. For all you know, Luiz could be planning to cast you aside once he's fulfilled the legal requirements of his father's will.

The perfect formula for revenge? He walks away from you the way you walked away from him seven years ago

Her stomach wanted to perform somersaults. She wanted to run to the bathroom to be sick in the nearest receptacle. She knew Luiz; she knew what he was capable of. And she suddenly remembered his scorpion. It was sitting there right in front of her now, crawling down the mirror as if ready to strike.

'*Señorita?*' Abril's voice sounded concerned. Could she see that Caroline was about to lose every ounce of courage she possessed in one huge wave of guilt?

'*Señorita…*' A gentle hand covered her forearm, the fingers small and brown against her own pale skin. 'You are shivering,' the little maid murmured worriedly. 'Are you frightened, *señorita?* Please don't be frightened,' she urged her comfortingly. '*El conde* is a good man. Everyone in the valley says so. He reminds them of his grandpa, Don Angeles. He was a good man also. A strong man.'

'I'm okay.' Caroline managed to push out the whisper. 'I just…' She shivered again, as if something scaly had walked over her flesh.

With a blink she attempted to pull herself together, shifting her gaze to her little maid of honour, who was standing beside her in a simple gown of virginal white. She looked enchanting. The perfect foil for a fair-skinned bride, with her black hair and black doe-like eyes and her beautiful olive skin.

'I'm fine,' she assured her for a second time, and even managed a smile.

Reassured, Abril handed Caroline her small bouquet of ivory roses, picked only an hour ago from the garden and woven together by Abril herself.

Her father was pacing restlessly in the great hall when he first saw her. He stopped dead and watched as she came down the stairs towards him. 'Goodness, Caro,' he murmured thickly, and that was all. The rest was written in his eyes.

She was surprised to find that it wasn't Vito who was going to drive her to the village, since Vito rarely left her side. But this time it was a stranger who drove Luiz's black BMW. She discovered why Vito had forsaken her only when she entered the church on her father's arm.

For Vito was standing next to Luiz. A Luiz who filled her heart with tears of relief when she saw him standing there in his black tuxedo, his dark head lowered and with a waiting tension clamped across his broad shoulders that made her want to sob with relief—because surely that tension meant this moment was important to him—that *she* was important?

There was a stir as people began glancing round at her; the stir brought up his head. He turned, looked at her— and that was the last thing she remembered for most of the long service. For no man could look at a woman like that unless he was seeing the only person he wanted to spend the rest of his life with. And his hand when it accepted hers from her father was even trembling slightly.

They made their vows in a hushed atmosphere where no one present seemed to breathe. But when Luiz slid not one but two rings onto her wedding finger she blinked, focused for the first time in ages, and saw a simple but exquisite diamond ring resting next to a finely sculptured gold band. She felt her eyes fill with tears.

For this was no ordinary betrothal ring, it was, in fact, her mother's ring. She glanced up into intensely black eyes. Luiz saw the tears and bent to whisper hoarsely. 'Don't...'

It was almost her complete undoing. Then Padre Domingo spoke. 'If you would place the ring on Don Luiz's finger, we can continue...'

Outside in the sunshine the villagers had gathered to

applaud them. Caroline clung to Luiz as if she had been joined to him in more ways than marriage just now. She blushed and smiled and was aware of Vito standing like a mountain beside the tiny Abril, of her father looking rather sombre and drawn. She was even aware of Tía Consuela, standing cool and erect—seeing the whole thing through to its bleak finish like a martyr to her chosen fate.

But Felipe was nowhere. Neither did he turn up when they sat down at the banquet table, now decked out with white linen and the kind of china and silverware that belonged in a museum.

Her hand had not been allowed to leave Luiz's once since he had formally claimed it. Even now, while they sat at the table, they were having to eat one-handed while their entwined fingers lay on the table between them.

'Thank you for this,' she said, catching sight of her mother's ring shining like a prism on her finger. 'What made you think of it?'

'It should have been *my* mother's ring,' he murmured quietly, looking down at the ring also. 'But she never had one so I went for the next best thing and asked your father for your mother's ring. He brought it back to Marbella with him, ready cleaned and altered to fit your finger...'

'Well, thank you,' she repeated huskily. 'It made everything just perfect.'

'No.' Looking up, Luiz caught her eyes with a look that set her head spinning. 'You are what makes everything perfect,' he said, and kissed her gently.

The gathered assembly began clapping, halting something else that felt absolutely perfect.

By the time they retired outside the sun had set and the garden was ablaze with twinkling lights. Luiz drew her into his arms on the makeshift dance floor as a small set of musicians began playing a waltz. It was the closest they had been except for the clasped hands since they had married, and the knowledge of that sparked between them. Electric, tantalising, utterly mesmerising.

His mouth brushed her cheek, then stayed there. 'You look so beautiful today. Walking towards me in the church, you made my heart ache,' he murmured huskily.

When she tilted her head back so she could look at him, her eyes had stars in them. But she paled a little when she remembered how she had been feeling earlier, and—more importantly—why she had felt like that. 'I've been talking to my father,' she murmured huskily. 'He told me what really happened seven years ago. I—'

The man holding her suddenly changed into an entirely different person. Seeing it happen stopped her words, and she watched his hardened eyes flick around the garden in angry search.

'Luiz—'

'No,' he cut in. 'I am angry with him for breaking his word to me and telling you all of this. I am angry with you for bringing it up tonight of all nights!'

'But you didn't take a single penny from him!' It had to be said! 'You left me asleep in bed each night and went down to play cards with him to stop him gambling with anyone else. You knew how I worried about him—so you took it upon yourself to keep him out of danger! I *owe* so much to you for that, Luiz!'

His face was white, his lips thin, his teeth clenched behind them. 'You owe me nothing,' he rasped.

'I owe you an apology,' she said thickly, beginning to tremble in his arms as the full cup of her guilt came pouring out. 'I was in love with you. I should have known you wouldn't do something so crass as to fleece my own father! But I believed him instead of you—when I *knew* what a liar he was! I don't blame you if you *never* forgive me for that!'

'Drop it, Caroline, before I get angry,' he warned.

But he was already angry. 'You let him win thousands from you—the same thousands of pounds he then told me you had won from him! It's no wonder he was so eager to play you again last week,' she said bitterly. 'He truly believed he was in for another easy killing!'

He flinched as if she'd struck him hard. 'I didn't mean it like that!' she groaned, lifting her hand to lay it in apology against his taut cheek. 'Luiz—'

'No,' he said. 'We will not discuss this. Not now, not ever. Do you understand?' And he took hold of her hand to remove it, then stepped right back, turned and walked away!

It was fortunate that the music had come to a stop just then. Luiz's knack for perfect timing, she supposed.

His uncle Fidel took his place. And after that Caroline didn't see him as she was whirled around in the arms of one relative or another. When she did eventually escape the dance floor to go and look for him it was pitch dark beyond the fairylights, while the castle itself was pooled in lamplight.

She couldn't find him amongst the people in the garden, so she went looking for him inside. She was just crossing the great hall when a waiter came up to her. 'Excuse me, *la condesa*.' He bowed politely. 'But *el conde* send me with a message.'

Oh, the relief. 'Where is he?' she asked urgently.

'He say to meet him at the car, just beyond the boundary wall, if you please.'

At the car? What now? she wondered as she moved out of the house again and down the driveway to where all the cars had been left parked outside the castle's boundary. Was she about to be hijacked again and hauled off somewhere else?

Well, if Luiz thought that was going to be a punishment, then he was in for a surprise, she thought, with a smile that took the anxiety from her lips as excitement for the game began to curl through her.

The car was just a dark bulk among many cars, but she picked it out soon enough because it was the only one with its engine running, and she caught a glimpse of Luiz's dark shape behind the wheel just before she opened the passenger door and slipped inside.

'This is all excitingly clandestine, Luiz,' she teased, busily tucking her dress and veil inside before she could close the door. 'But not really necessary any more.' The door closed, the engine gunned, then shot them forwards. 'See,' she said, turning to wave her ringed hand at him. 'I am...'

Words died, and so did her heart, just before it dropped with a sickening thump to her stomach. As she made a lurch for the door handle the central locking system clicked smoothly into place and Felipe turned a lazy grin on her.

'Droit du seigneur,' he drawled. 'It is tradition...'

CHAPTER ELEVEN

HER first instinct was to begin looking wildly about her, to see if anyone had seen them speed away. But there was no one else on this side of the wall to witness their departure, and as Felipe accelerated up the road towards the village her mind was already hearing the smooth, quiet run of the car's powerful engine.

'This is stupid, Felipe,' she said, trying to keep the need to panic under control. 'I don't see what you aim to gain by it.'

'Satisfaction,' he replied, and turned an abrupt right. Instead of taking the road through the village he began driving at speed between the narrow rows of fruit trees. It was a hair-raising experience, one that had Caroline clinging to the door handle, her body flinching each time a tree branch scraped across the car.

Another abrupt turn and they were skirting the side of the valley on a dusty track she hadn't even known was there. Within what seemed like only seconds they had skirted round the village and were climbing through the terraces. With her heart pumping so fast with adrenaline that her hands were trembling, Caroline reached for the seat belt and fastened it around her.

'You're mad,' she breathed.

Felipe just shrugged, spun the car round one of the acute bends in the narrow road and for a few brief moments brought the whole valley into view. She could see the castle, pooled in light and standing out against its dramatic black backdrop. She could even see the people dancing on the makeshift dance floor, or just standing around in groups, talking. Her heart began to throb, her throat to thicken as she tried to pick out Luiz's distinctive figure—before Felipe was swinging them sharply in the other direction.

By the next abrupt turn the castle was far below them, and it was a shock to realise how high they had already climbed. Another couple of these sharp bends and they would reach the cut, the place where the road became a treacherous pass through the mountains.

She didn't want to go there with Felipe. She didn't want this madman driving her at this mad speed on that awful part of the road where the edge dropped sheer down hundreds of feet into the ravines below.

'Stop the car, Felipe,' she commanded shakily. 'A joke is a joke, and if it makes you feel better, I'll admit it—I'm frightened. But now I would like you to stop so I can get out.'

'And walk back?' he mocked. 'In that dress and in those spindly heels?'

'Yes, if necessary.' She didn't care so long as he let her out of here.

They suddenly swung around yet another sharp bend. Tyres screamed and spun. Caroline hung on for dear life and almost cried out when all she could see in front of her was what looked like a wall of pitch black.

Her heart leapt into her throat and remained there until she realised they weren't about to drive off the end of the mountain but were in actual fact heading straight for it.

'I will have been missed by now.' In sheer desperation she tried another tack. 'Luiz's car will have been missed. He will be coming after us as we speak. Do you think he won't have noticed the car lights as we've climbed? Drop me off now, Felipe and you will have a chance to get away! Keep going and he will catch up to us and kill you, I swear it!'

'Starting to panic a bit, aren't you?' He grinned—and swung them round yet another acute turn in the road.

He did it so carelessly that it actually threw her hard against his shoulder. By the time she had righted herself again she was looking at stars glinting between two towering black walls, and realised in horror that they had now reached the mountain pass.

'Felipe!' she cried out shrilly. 'Stop this—stop it!'

But he wasn't going to stop anything. Not the car, not his wild and reckless driving, not the stupidity that was making him behave like this.

'It might be an interesting form of revenge to see Luiz's face when he finds you way down there in the ravine amongst the tangled wreckage of his very own car,' he murmured tauntingly.

Then he laughed as Caroline's face went white.

'But I am not quite that hungry,' he said. 'My original plan suits my idea of revenge a lot better.'

'I don't know w-what you're talking about,' she stammered, through tense teeth that were beginning to chatter.

'Yes, you do,' he argued. 'You are from the right stock to know all about ancient tribal rites. If you just think of me as the rightful owner of what we have just left behind, then the whole experience could be quite exciting—a bride on her wedding night who finds herself sleeping with the lord of the castle, rather than the peasant she married herself to.'

'Luiz is not the peasant around here,' Caroline tossed back. 'And if you think I would let any other man but Luiz touch me, you are sadly mistaken.'

'So you are pretending to be in love with the bastard,' he drawled, eyeing her curiously. 'Why? Does it make it easier to let him touch you when you can close your eyes and see *el conde* instead of a New York thug?'

'I don't need to pretend. I *do* love Luiz,' she declared.

'And will you keep your eyes on the road?' she choked out when he took them swerving round a deep curve in the road with scant regard for what might be on the other side of it.

'Stop worrying,' he said. 'I've been driving this road since I was a teenager. I know every twist and rut in it from here to Cordoba.'

Caroline could only hope and pray that was true! One of her hands had fixed itself to the car door handle; the other was clutching the strap of her seat belt. Felipe took in her taut posture—and recklessly swung the car round yet another curve.

She closed her eyes, unable to watch any more.

'You married him because he offered to pay off your father's debts if you did.' He calmly returned to the other subject. 'It had nothing to do with love.'

'I married Luiz because I can't bear to be without him,' Caroline countered through tightly gritted teeth.

'Liar,' he jeered. 'You were bought! Bought with his money. Bought with his name. Bought by the bastard of Don Carlos Vazquez,' he spat out scathingly. 'And you are prepared to lie in his bed and close your sweet English eyes to his low beginnings, his prostitute *mamá* and the questionable way he earned his millions. Because it is better to close your eyes and pretend he is Don Luiz Vazquez *el conde* rather than the crook that stole from his own family!'

'Luiz didn't steal from you.'

'He stole my title!' he rasped. 'He stole my money and my home! He stole what was my God-given right from birth!'

His fist hit the steering wheel in sheer anger. Caroline flinched, and began praying fervently that they made it round the next bend.

'But I will steal one thing back from him before I leave

here for ever,' Felipe continued thinly. 'I will steal his wedding night,' he vowed. 'And my reward will be in knowing that *he* will know every time he looks at you that it was me who had his beautiful wife first!'

'Luiz and I have been lovers for years!' She laughed at the sheer idiocy of what he was saying. 'You can't steal what he has already had!'

'His wedding night, I can,' he insisted grimly.

This was crazy. *He* was crazy! 'You stole from *him*, Felipe!' Caroline contended shrilly. 'It was not the other way around! You aren't even his half-brother! Your mother is a cheat and a liar, and she tricked her own sister out of Don Carlos's life so that she could take her place. She set up a situation and used it ruthlessly to her own ends. She twisted everything around so that it appeared that Luiz's mother had been sleeping with *her* married lover! Then your mother stepped neatly into the breach left by her sister—having first made sure that Serena had safely disappeared to America with her unborn child!'

'That is a lie!' he barked. The car swerved precariously. Caroline's heart leapt to her throat and stayed there while she clung on for dear life.

Don't argue with him! she told herself frantically. Ignore him and just let him get you down this wretched mountain in one whole piece!

But she couldn't seem to stop the words from coming. They burst forth from the cold dark place she had been keeping them hidden ever since she had read the full horrible truth about the Vazquez family.

'A few months later your mother married Don Carlos— with *her* lover's child already spawned in her belly. That child was you, Felipe,' she persisted, quoting almost verbatim Luiz's father's own wretched words. 'Your real father was Don Carlos's best friend. His *married* friend!' she declared. 'And the moment you opened your eyes on the morning you were born he saw his best friend looking back at him and knew——*knew* he had been tricked and used and betrayed by your mother to secure her own future at the expense of her sister's! Since that same day Luiz has always been his father's heir and you have never been led to think otherwise!'

'How the hell do you know all of this?' Felipe rasped, beginning, for the first time, to sound choked by his own wretched lies.

'From Don Carlos himself,' she said. 'He kept detailed diaries of everything that happened, including the years he spent looking for Serena and his true son *and* the fact that he never kept any of this secret from you.'

'I hated the bastard,' Felipe gritted. 'He spent thirty-four years of my life mourning a son he never knew while I was right there, waiting to be loved if he could only see it!'

'He was wrong to treat you like that,' Caroline acknowledged. 'But two wrongs don't make a right, Felipe! And what you are doing here now is wrong——can't you see that?'

She hoped she was getting through to him. She hoped that she could make him see sense, maybe even turn them around and take her back again!

But he suddenly growled out the kind of curse that said a monster had taken over his soul right now, and with a lurch he threw them round another corner, sending the headlamps scanning out across a terrible nothingness that locked a silent scream into Caroline's throat.

They hit a deep rut in the road. The scream found full voice as Felipe began to struggle with the wheel. He was cursing and cursing, and she was screaming, and the car was careering all over the place.

They were going to die; she was sure of it! They were going to tumble off the edge of the cliff and never be

found! Sheer terror made her grab hold of the handbrak(
Sheer terror made her yank it on hard. On a squeal of h(
rubber the car gave a lurch, then began skidding sideway(
while she sat there and watched in open-eyed horror a
they slid closer and closer to the edge of the ravine.

Then they hit something solid—a rock on the edge? Sh(
didn't know, but they began lurching back the way the(
had come. Then, just when she thought the car was goin(
to stop safely, it hit something else, made a terrible groa(
and toppled very gently onto its side.

Shocked and dizzyingly disorientated, Caroline sat for
few moments, not actually remembering where she was
Then her head began to hurt, and it all came flooding sick(
eningly back as she lifted her fingers to gently touch th(
sore area by her temple, realising that she must have h(
her head and been knocked out for a while.

Most definitely frightened of what she might find, sh(
turned to look at Felipe. He was at the very least uncor(
scious, sitting hunched over the steering wheel and slightl(
below her because of the drunken angle of the car.

Carefully, fearfully almost, she reached out and touche(
her fingers to his neck. She could feel living warmth ther(
and a shimmer of a pulse. 'Oh, thank God,' she breathe(
out shakily. She closed her eyes and said it again. 'Than(
God.'

What now? Where are we? How badly placed are w(
regarding the ravine? What do I do?

It was then she realised that the car headlights were sti(
burning. With the greatest of care she tried edging hersel(
forward so she could peer out of the car windscreen. (
was a miracle it hadn't shattered, she supposed. Beyond
she could just make out in the lights good solid road an(
the ravine edge, way over to her right.

They must have keeled over into a ditch near the moun(
tain, she realised. And it was such a relief to know it tha(

she relaxed back in the seat with a sigh and took a few moments to let her heart-rate steady before she attempted to get out.

Felipe had locked the doors, she remembered. But surely there was something somewhere she could pull or push to make them unlock again? With shaky fingers scrambling over pitch black metal and leather, she managed to find something on the door that felt as if it would pull up, tugged it and heard the lock spring free.

Next she had to release the seat belt. Then came the tricky bit, opening the car door and keeping it open while she attempted to scramble out. Her dress snagged on something; she heard it rip and lost her shoes in the struggle. But eventually she landed in a heap on the hard road, then just sat slumped there while she got her breath back.

It was all so quiet, so eerie. She shivered, then suddenly couldn't stop shivering—though she didn't think it was because it was that cold up here.

Shock, she presumed. I'm probably shocked. And who wouldn't be after the ordeal I've just had?

The last thought brought a smile to her lips. The smile made her feel better, and she scrambled up on her bare feet and began to take careful stock of the situation.

Felipe obviously needed help; that was her first consideration. But help was either ten miles or so down the mountain or five miles or so back the way they had come. Not much of a choice, really, she mused helplessly. Staying put seemed to make better sense. Someone should have missed her by now, surely?

Never mind merely *someone,* she then scolded herself. Luiz should have missed her!

It was then that she heard it. It was nothing more at the moment than a very distant growl. But it was a car engine, she recognised, fading in and out as it wound round the mountain.

In sheer relief she simply sank to the ground by the drunken car, folded her now aching head onto her knees and wrapped them in her trembling arms.

It had to be Luiz coming to find her. She didn't ever let herself think that it might be anyone else. In fact, that was the most stupid part of Felipe's plan of abduction—to actually believe he could just drive away with her without having Luiz hard on his tail. Had he truly believed he would get as far as seduction? The crazy idiot. If she knew Luiz, the road off the mountain towards Los Aminos was probably blocked by now anyway. Felipe would have been stopped before he'd even got started.

The car was coming closer; she could hear the smooth, neat way it was being driven into the bends and corners—could even pick out the gear changes, the braking, the steady increase in speed then the smooth throttling back.

Yet he arrived round the final bend without warning. Odd that, she thought, as she lifted her head and just watched as he brought the strange car to a standstill perhaps ten feet away.

He didn't get out of the car immediately, either. He just sat there with the headlights trained on her and, she presumed, looked at her looking at him.

Then his door came open. His feet scraped on gravel. And, finally, the full lean length of his body appeared. She couldn't see his face—well, she could have done if she'd looked at it, but for some unaccountable reason she just didn't want to.

He walked towards her. Stopped about two feet away and took a look around their remote surroundings. It was so quiet up here you could hear an ant move a leaf. The sky was a navy blue star-studded cloth and the mountains soared like giants standing on guard.

'Where is he?' was the first question he asked her, and he did it softly, with no inflexion whatsoever.

'Unconscious,' she replied. 'In the car.'

Luiz nodded. That was all, no further questions. He didn't even take a look at Felipe. With a flick of his fingers all the other doors flew open on the car he had been driving. Three men got out; one of them was Vito. They came towards them.

'Deal with him,' he said.

Caroline felt her blood turn cold. 'No, Luiz,' she protested, having visions of poor Felipe being thrown off the edge of the mountain. 'He's hurt. He needs help. I...'

Swooping down, he gathered her into his arms and straightened. He began striding back to the car he had arrived in, and Caroline had a ludicrous vision of herself in all her bridal finery, now ripped and soiled, with her pretty lace veil trailing on the dusty ground behind them.

It was only when they reached the open passenger door that she let herself dare look into Luiz's face. What she saw there brought the first tears to her eyes since the whole ordeal had begun.

'Don't,' she whispered unsteadily. 'Don't shut me out.'

He didn't respond, just placed her in the car then walked round to climb in beside her. The engine fired and then they were moving, continuing down the mountain, because even she could see that it was too narrow here to turn the car around.

As they passed the drunken BMW she saw Vito heaving Felipe out of the car by using sheer brute strength. But he was gentle when he laid him out on the road to check him over. It was faintly reassuring to see that gentleness. Surely men like Vito would not be gentle with a man they were intending to tip over the edge of a mountain, she consoled herself.

A half-mile further on Luiz stopped the car where the road was a little wider and turned them back the way they had come. As they passed by the BMW again, she noticed that another car had pulled up behind it and that Felipe was on his own two feet, leaning weakly against it with his head in his hands, while the rest of the men were wrestling the BMW out of harm's way.

'They won't hurt him, will they?' she asked Luiz anxiously.

'No,' was all he said.

It was reassuring, short though it was. On a small sigh she began to shiver. Luiz instantly flicked the car heater on, but the shivering continued. She knew it was shock not cold—Luiz probably knew it too.

'Tell me what happened after that fool of a waiter let Felipe convince him he was me so he could lure you out to my car.'

'When you start shouting and swearing, I might tell you,' Caroline countered dully. 'But not before.'

'All right.' His fingers tensed around the steering wheel. 'Let's just deal with your problem with my self-control first,' he clipped. 'You want to see the man dead?' he gritted. 'You want to see his head hanging from the castle wall? You want to see me drive you up this mountain the same way he brought you down it?'

'No.' She answered all of his questions at the same time.

'Then tell me what happened after he got you into my car,' he repeated flatly.

So, quietly and as flatly as him, she told him everything, even the way it had been her fault that the car had ended up where it had. The only bit she missed out was the hellish row she and Felipe had had about Luiz's father.

By then they were driving through the village and everyone was out. It was like a replay of the first time they had come through here. Only then it had been daylight and the expressions had been curious. Now they looked pale and worried and anxious. So she waved and smiled and hoped to goodness they couldn't tell that she was just about ready to cry her eyes out.

It was the same when they got back to the castle. Everyone was huddled around Neptune, waiting with anxious eyes as Luiz brought the car to a stop then grimly told her to stay exactly where she was.

He got out, ignored everyone, and came around the car to lift her out of her seat. Some gasped when they saw the state of her lovely dress and her pale face.

Her father stepped up and took hold of her hand. He looked dreadful. 'I'm fine,' she told him, and another one of those reassuring smiles appeared.

'You don't look it,' he rasped.

'Well, I am—I am,' she repeated firmly.

'Nevertheless, I will come with you…'

It was Luiz's uncle Fidel. He fell into step beside Luiz as they walked into the great hall with her father still clinging to one of her hands. The first person she saw inside was Consuela. She was just standing there by the huge banqueting table, her face so white it could have been marble.

'Put me down, Luiz,' Caroline insisted.

He paused in his step but didn't immediately comply.

'Please,' she pleaded.

Without a word, and with his dark face still that tightly closed book, he set her feet onto the cool stone floor and made sure she was steady before letting go of her. Caroline walked up to Consuela and simply—sadly—just put her arms around the older woman.

Instantly Consuela stiffened so violently that Caroline thought it was with rejection. Then she realised, as that stiff body began to tremble, that Consuela just wasn't used to being held in any way. For all she had deserved punishment for what she had done to her own sister, she had paid for it—with thirty-five years of a barren marriage living in a barren atmosphere where love and affection had been non-existent.

'It's all right,' she whispered, for the other woman's ears only. 'He's fine. Luiz's men are looking after him.'

'He should not have done it,' Consuela said, but some of the tension eased out of her.

'He's bitter,' Caroline explained. 'And he has a right to be bitter, Tía Consuela,' she added gently.

The older woman looked into Caroline's face and sighed knowingly. 'The *padre* gave you the diaries,' she said.

At Caroline's nod, she nodded also. That was all. They understood each other. If Caroline had read the diaries then she knew that if Luiz thought his life had been hard, growing up in the slums of New York, then Felipe's life had been no easier, living here with a father who had despised him and a mother who had locked herself away in an emotional prison of her own making.

Then Consuela said. 'We will leave here tonight.' It was a decision that made Caroline glance at her anxiously.

'You don't have to do that, Consuela,' she told her. 'This is your home. It's Felipe's home. Can't we at least try to live here together?'

'No.' Consuela shook her head. 'In truth, I will be glad to go. It is time. Perhaps...' She heaved out a heavy sigh. 'Perhaps more than time that we began making a life for ourselves.'

In a lot of ways Caroline could only agree with her. Felipe, at least, needed to get away from here. It was the only way he would learn to put aside his bitterness.

The sound of another car arriving alerted Caroline to the return of the others, and her immediate concern turned to getting Luiz away from the hall before his men brought Felipe into it.

Releasing Consuela, she turned back to Luiz. He looked so big and grim that she felt the threat of tears tighten her chest muscles as she walked back to him. She turned impulsively to Luiz's uncle. 'Felipe will need you more than I do, Tío,' she told him.

There was a moment when he looked as if he might argue with her, then with a glance at Luiz he changed his mind and nodded. To her father she gave a hug and a kiss. 'I'll see you tomorrow,' she said quietly.

He too understood. He was being dismissed. Standing back, he watched her slip her hand into Luiz's hand, saw the larger fingers tighten possessively around her more slender ones, and together the two of them moved up the stairs.

Behind them, not a single word was spoken.

Instead of to her old room Luiz took her directly to his. It was the master suite of the castle. Huge. Grand. All heavy baroque furniture and ancient artefacts. The moment the door shut behind them Caroline felt reaction begin to set in.

Her legs felt suddenly weak, sending her over to the nearest chair to drop shakily down into it. Still without a word, Luiz walked across the room and into his bathroom. Ten seconds later she could hear the sound of running water.

Coming back into the room, Luiz found her sitting there, with her face hidden in her hands. A muscle along his jaw clenched, but that was the only reaction he showed as he came to stand over her, then bent to gently remove the tiara and veil from her hair before scooping her into his arms again.

'Oh, very macho,' she said, trying to lighten the leaden atmosphere.

He didn't respond to it. Grim-eyed, tight-lipped, he carried her into the bathroom, then set her down on her feet and turned her back to him so he could begin untying the silk lacing that was holding the bodice of her wedding dress together.

'If you don't start talking to me, I'll throw a tantrum,' she informed him quite casually. The lacing gave, the bodice slipped, sending her hand up to catch it before it revealed her breasts.

'Luiz!' she snapped, spinning round to face him.

His eyes caught fire. The fury he had been keeping severely banked down now came bursting out through those hot, bright, burning black eyes to completely envelop her at the very moment his arms did the same. And he was lifting her off her feet, so he could bring her startled mouth on a level with his own mouth.

It was a kiss like no other. It didn't just burn, it consumed. Her arms went up, slender forearms using his wide shoulders as a brace to keep that fierce mouth-to-mouth contact. She didn't care now that the dress was slipping, that her breasts were bursting free to press against him. She didn't care that the knock on her head hurt or that her bare feet were stinging or that he was holding her so tightly that he was in danger of crushing her ribs.

But she cared that she could feel him trembling, that even his mouth, where it fused with hers, was struggling to maintain some control over what was finally pouring out of him.

'I love you,' she murmured through a fevered grab at air. 'I love you so much, and I hate it when you hide away from me!'

'It's either hide or devour you,' he muttered. And he meant it, fantastic though the statement might seem. He meant every harsh, rasping word of it.

He claimed her mouth again, putting a stop to any more talking, because at this moment *doing* was more important. Caroline wound her thighs around his hips, long skirts rustling as she locked her bare feet together at his back. Her fingers were in his hair, her thumbs urgently caressing the tension along his rigid jaw.

On a driven groan he turned back to the bedroom.

'The bath,' she reminded him.

He issued a hoarse curse against her lips and changed direction without breaking the heated contact of their mouths until he absolutely had to. But he refused to let go of her as he bent to turn off the taps. And when he straightened again she was waiting for him, flushed-cheeked, misty-eyed, the two creamy slopes of her breasts heaving against the boned bodice now resting beneath them.

His dark lashes floated downward as he looked her over. She looked delectably pagan, uninhibitedly wanton. A bride ready for the taking by her passionate Spanish husband.

Looking upwards again, he studied her soft, full, inviting mouth, pressed another claiming kiss to it, then let his eyes clash with hers. He was moving again. Back into the bedroom, across the priceless Indian carpet covering its solid oak floor, to the bed, which looked like an island you could quite easily live upon without needing to leave for a long, long time.

Caroline certainly didn't want to leave it. She wanted to take off her clothes and crawl beneath its snowy white linen topped by the really decadent blood-red and dark gold brocade coverlet, to survive on hot kisses and rich dark flesh and the passions of a man who was incomparable.

Allowing her feet to slide to the floor, Luiz took a step back, then began undressing. She didn't move, didn't attempt to take her own dress off. That was for him to do. It was his duty to unwrap his bride himself.

But her breasts pouted provocatively at him all the while he was undressing, and the moist pink tip of her tongue kept snaking slowly around her kiss-swollen lips in needy anticipation.

'You,' he murmured when he eventually reached for her, 'ought to be locked up.'

She just smiled a very wicked smile and lifted up her arms to receive him. The dress slipped lower. On a growl, Luiz helped it the rest of the way, and had seen off everything else she was wearing before he straightened up again.

Outside, beyond the four-foot thick walls, the party went on without them. Somewhere else, in another wing of the castle, two people were packing.

'Luiz...' Caroline murmured tentatively a long time later, when they lay curled up against each other. 'Can we talk?' she begged. 'About Felipe?'

It ruined the moment. His body went taut, his jawline clenched. 'Only if we have to do,' he said tightly—which didn't offer much encouragement.

Caroline pushed on anyway. 'I know you have every right to hate him and his mother,' she allowed. 'And I know he behaved appallingly tonight. But...' Leaning up a little, she looked anxiously into his ice-cold eyes. 'It isn't his fault his mother told wicked lies about your mother, or that she tricked and deceived your father! Just as it isn't Felipe's fault that you had the childhood you did. He *is* your cousin—and it's been tough for him too, you know!' she insisted at Luiz's lowering frown. 'Growing up in your shadow, with a mother who could barely live with herself for what she'd done to her own sister and a so-called father who rejected him at birth and hated his mother for putting him in your place. It's all so very tragic and sad,' she said. 'And I know your father had a right to feel bitter as he wrote it. He broke his own heart by believing your aunt instead of your mother, and spent the rest of his life punishing himself for it. But Felipe should not have been made to pay. It—'

'What do you mean—how my father *wrote* it?' Luiz put in.

'Oh!' she gasped in horror when she realised what she'd said. Then a long sigh whispered from her, and with a twisted smile that acknowledged it was probably for the best she lifted sombre eyes to his darkly glowering ones. 'How he wrote it in his diaries,' she said gently.

Softly and quietly she began telling him everything she had learned.

When eventually Luiz asked her where the diaries were, she told him, and without another word he got out of bed, pulled on a robe and went to get them.

A long time later, on his way back from Caroline's bedroom, he saw Felipe and his mother just about to leave the castle. Standing there on the upper gallery, he viewed their sober features and felt something pick at the stone it was reputed he had for a heart.

'Felipe,' he said. The other man's dark head came up and he spun on his heel to glance upwards. 'We need to talk,' he murmured quietly.

Instantly Luiz could see the battle taking place behind the defensive aggression pasted onto his handsome features. Then, on a sigh, Felipe gave a curt nod of his head. 'One day,' he replied. Maybe he, like Luiz, had had enough of the lies and bitterness and betrayal. 'One day...' he repeated, and turned away again.

Luiz watched gravely as his aunt lifted her pale face up to him. 'I'm sorry,' was all she said, but Luiz understood. After all, what else could she add that could take away what had gone before?

When he went back into his bedroom, he found his bride no longer there. Tossing the diaries onto the tumbled bed, he went looking for her and found her soaking in a bath of steaming bubbles. It took him ten seconds to join her, uncaringly sloshing water over the rim onto the tiled floor as he climbed in behind her then sat down and drew her back against him.

'I've just seen Felipe and my aunt leaving,' he told her levelly.

Caroline nodded. 'She told me they would leave tonight.'

'I didn't want them to do that.' He sighed. 'I never meant to actually throw them out of here. Family is family...'

'Warts and all?' She nodded, 'I know,' she said referring to her own feckless father. Picking up one of his hands, she began kissing his fingers. 'Did you read the diaries?' she asked.

'Mmm.' His other hand slid up her slippery flesh until it found and closed around one of her breasts. 'I knew some of it,' he confessed. 'First from my mother and then from my father, when we did eventually attempt to communicate.'

'Seven years ago,' Catherine sighed out bleakly, thinking of all those years they'd lost.

'Seven years ago,' he agreed. 'When I made the trip to Spain to arrogantly lay claim to my roots and met the woman who claimed me instead.'

'I'm sorry,' she said, thinking about how ruthlessly her father had used one of them against the other.

'I told your father that I was in love with you and wanted to marry you,' he informed her heavily. 'He politely informed me where I could go. I wasn't good enough for his daughter, he said. At the time I agreed with him.' He grimaced. 'Still do, actually.'

'But you'll have me anyway,' Caroline added smilingly. 'There really isn't much to pick between you, my father and poor Felipe,' she said. 'You're all too self-motivated to be true.'

'Felipe was right when he compared my father's life with the life of the ancestor who built this castle,' Luiz remarked gruffly. 'It was history repeating itself.'

Twisting in the water until she was facing him, Caroline murmured softly, 'Not this time, though. This time the Conde got his woman. That makes for a happy ending.'

Eyes like dark chasms filled with satisfaction. 'A very happy ending,' Luiz agreed huskily, and began to kiss her...

Tyler Brides

It happened one weekend...

Quinn and Molly Spencer are delighted to accept three
bookings for their newly opened B&B, Breakfast Inn Bed,
located in America's favorite hometown, Tyler, Wisconsin.

But Gina Santori is anything but thrilled to discover her
best friend has tricked her into sharing a room with
the man who broke her heart eight years ago....

And Delia Mayhew can hardly believe that she's
gotten herself locked in the Breakfast Inn Bed
basement with the sexiest man in America.

Then there's Rebecca Salter. She's turned up at the
Inn in her wedding gown. Minus her groom.

*Come home to Tyler for three delightful novellas
by three of your favorite authors: Kristine Rolofson,
Heather MacAllister and Jacqueline Diamond.*

HARLEQUIN®
Makes any time special ™

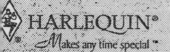

HARLEQUIN®

makes any time special—online...

eHARLEQUIN.com

shop eHarlequin

- ♥ Find all the new Harlequin releases at everyday great discounts.
- ♥ Try before you buy! Read an excerpt from the latest Harlequin novels.
- ♥ Write an online review and share your thoughts with others.

reading room

- ♥ Read our Internet exclusive daily and weekly online serials, or vote in our interactive novel.
- ♥ Talk to other readers about your favorite novels in our Reading Groups.
- ♥ Take our Choose-a-Book quiz to find the series that matches you!

authors' alcove

- ♥ Find out interesting tidbits and details about your favorite authors' lives, interests and writing habits.
- ♥ Ever dreamed of being an author? Enter our Writing Round Robin. The Winning Chapter will be published online! Or review our writing guidelines for submitting your novel.

If you enjoyed what you just read,
then we've got an offer you can't resist!

Take 2 bestselling love stories FREE!

Plus get a FREE surprise gift!

Clip this page and mail it to Harlequin Reader Service®

IN U.S.A.
3010 Walden Ave.
P.O. Box 1867
Buffalo, N.Y. 14240-1867

IN CANADA
P.O. Box 609
Fort Erie, Ontario
L2A 5X3

YES! Please send me 2 free Harlequin Presents® novels and my free surprise gift. Then send me 6 brand-new novels every month, which I will receive months before they're available in stores. In the U.S.A., bill me at the bargain price of $3.34 plus 25¢ delivery per book and applicable sales tax, if any*. In Canada, bill me at the bargain price of $3.74 plus 25¢ delivery per book and applicable taxes**. That's the complete price and a savings of at least 10% off the cover prices—what a great deal! I understand that accepting the 2 free books and gift places me under no obligation ever to buy any books. I can always return a shipment and cancel at any time. Even if I never buy another book from Harlequin, the 2 free books and gift are mine to keep forever. So why not take us up on our invitation. You'll be glad you did!

106 HEN C22Q
306 HEN C22R

Name	(PLEASE PRINT)	
Address	Apt.#	
City	State/Prov.	Zip/Postal Code

* Terms and prices subject to change without notice. Sales tax applicable in N.Y.
** Canadian residents will be charged applicable provincial taxes and GST.
All orders subject to approval. Offer limited to one per household.
® are registered trademarks of Harlequin Enterprises Limited.

PRES00   ©1998 Harlequin Enterprises Limited

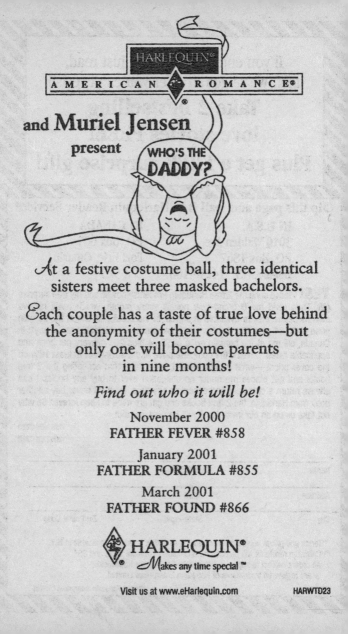

HARLEQUIN®

AMERICAN ◆ ROMANCE®

and **Muriel Jensen**

present

WHO'S THE
DADDY?

𝒜t a festive costume ball, three identical
sisters meet three masked bachelors.

�ℰach couple has a taste of true love behind
the anonymity of their costumes—but
only one will become parents
in nine months!

Find out who it will be!

November 2000
FATHER FEVER #858

January 2001
FATHER FORMULA #855

March 2001
FATHER FOUND #866

HARLEQUIN®
𝓜akes any time special ™

7-DAY LOAN

Stamp indicates date for return

This item may be renewed if not required by another customer

To renew, use the library catalogue or tel: 0113 343 5663

Fines will be charged for late returns

	Edward Boyle Library	
24-10-07		
31-10-07	WITHDRAWN	

Édition
annotée et c
Thanh-Vân TON-
Ancienne élève de l'E.N.S de Pari
Agrégée de Lettres modernes

www.petitsclassiques.com